My Living
HELL

My Living
HELL

JOSEPH E. COKER

Order this book online at www.trafford.com
or email orders@trafford.com

Most Trafford titles are also available at major online book retailers.

Printed in the United States of America.

ISBN: 978-1-4269-7171-6 (sc)
ISBN: 978-1-4269-7172-3 (hc)
ISBN: 978-1-4269-7173-0 (e)

Library of Congress Control Number: 2011909528

Trafford rev. 06/08/2011

 www.trafford.com

North America & International
toll-free: 1 888 232 4444 (USA & Canada)
phone: 250 383 6864 ♦ fax: 812 355 4082

Chapter 1
THE NIGHTMARE BEGINS

As he sat there watching the waves wash up on the beach. John's mind went back in time. To a part of his life that he would never forget but was very glad that it was over. He was thanking about how it all got started. How his mother hurt Sue and John after their father died." And trying to keep them from doing what they wanted to, do with their life. But now she was dead and John and Sue, is going on with their life. John had wanted to get into the Import-Export business and he knew that he won't be able to get the money that he would need by him self so he started to look for investers that was interested in investing in this type of business. So he placed some ads on a number of business websites. Telling investers about the business and that he needed five million dollars to get the business going. A week later he got a, email that was from a man named Parry Hanz. And that he was interested and would like more information about the business. So John emailed Mr. Hanz the business plan that he had wrote. Tuesday of the next week John got another email from Mr. Hanz saying that he liked the business plan and that he was wanting to invest in the business and sent John his telephone number asking John to call him so they could talk about the business. So John called Mr. Hanz the next day to talk to him about the investment. He tells John that he had forty two million that he wanted to invest in the business. John said I only need five million. Yes but that would help the company financially said Mr. Hanz. Ok when and where do you want to meet to sign the PPM and contracts and transfer the money asked John? Friday week and we will meet at your Attorney's office to sign the PPM and contracts and I will have the money transferred on Friday as well, said Mr. Hanz. John said ok I, will see you then bye. John started to run a back ground" check on Mr. Hanz to find out what he could about this man but he found nothing. But John was thanking to him self why would a man invest that much money in a start up business. On Tuesday of the next week Mr. Hanz calls John to see if he had made the arrangements at the bank. John said that everything was going as planed. Great said Mr. Hanz I was wondering if I can ask you something? Sure John said. Did you run a back" ground check on me asked Mr. Hanz. John said yes I did I always run a back, ground check on all investers that show interest in my business. Why is there something wrong John asked? No said Mr. Hanz I was just asking I will see you Friday morning. Ok said John bye. That Friday John got up and took a shower and got dressed and went out side to feed his cat muffin. When a man in a blue sedan came up and got out and asked if he was John Martin and John said that he was why? The man was very well dressed and was wearing gloves. John asked the man his name but the man wouldn't tell John his name. All he would tell John is that Mr. Hanz had change his mind about the investment and wanted his money back and he wanted it now. John told the man that the money hadn't been transferred yet. The man said yes it had and he wanted it now. John told him to leave and started back into the house and the man followed John into the house. John went and got his gun and they started to fight over the gun and it went off hitting John over the heart. The man thought that John was dead and left as fast as he could. A short time later John's sister Sue came up. She wanted to ask him over for dinner that night as she came up the drive way she seen that the door was open so she came in and saw John laying there in a pool of blood she went to the telephone and call 911. The EMS came as fast as they could and while they were working on John and putting him in the ambulance Sue was talking to the law. I am Lt. Smith of the Bellburg police what is your name and can you tell me what happen here. She held back the tears the best that she could and said that I am Sue Martin John's sister. I came over to see if he could come over for dinner tonight. When I came up I saw that the door was open so I came in and saw him laying" there so I called 911. Did you see anyone leaving the house asked Lt. Smith? Sue said no. Ok thank you miss Martin that will be all for now said Lt. Smith. So Sue left John's house and went to the Bellburg hospital where he was in surgery. Sue called Tracy and told her what happen to John.

Tracy met Sue at the hospital. Tracy asked Sue what happen and Sue said I don't know I went in and found him on the floor in a pool of blood only he knows what happen. John had been in surgery for about three hours. When Dr. Hampton came out and told Sue and Tracy that John had made it thru surgery but was in very crucial condition and was in ICU. Sue asked if they could see him. Yes only for a short time said Dr. Hampton. So Sue and Tracy went in to see John they had him a sleep and on life support. Sue looked at John and said what happen out there little brother. Tracy put her arm around Sue and said John is a fighter he is going to make it. Sue hugged around Tracy and said I hope so. Sue stayed at the hospital that night with John. The next morning Lt Smith came to see if he could talk to John but Sue told Lt. Smith that there was no change in John's condition. Lt. Smith told Sue that it look like John tried to kill him self. That only prints found on the gun was John's and the GSR was all over his hands. No one heard or seen any thing it is looking more and more like sucide to me. But we will get his story when he wakes up if he ever does. Sue looked at Lt. Smith and said with a very angry voice John didn't try to kill his self and he will pull thru and she started crying. He is all the family I have left. Lady lets hope you are right said the lieutenant. As he went to leave he told Dr. Hampton to call him when John got where he could talk and the doctor said he would. Dr. Hampton told Sue not to let that up set her that cops are just that way and to hope for the best. The doctor kept a close watch on John thru the night and by morning he was stronger. Dr. Hampton told Sue that John was getting stronger and that they was going to try to take him off of life support that afternoon. So Sue called Tracy to tell her what the doctor told her. And Tracy told Sue that she would be there with her. It was three in the afternoon when Dr. Hampton came into John's room and said ok folks here we go. Sue and Tracy was, there' by John's side as Dr. Hampton shut down the life support. Sue said come on little brother breathe you can do it yes. John was now breathing on, his own. Sue and Tracy hug one another

with tears of joy running down their face. Tracy looked at Sue and said he is going to be ok I told you he was a fighter he is going to be ok. Dr. Hampton looked at them both and said with a big smile he has come along way but he's not out of the woods yet. Sue stayed with John sleeping on a bed that the hospital gave her. The next morning Tracy came back to see John and to bring Sue something to eat. As they were talking John started to wake up. Tracy said come on open those big brown eyes come on that's it yes. Sue went and told the nurses and they came in and asked how he was feeling and was he in any pain. John said yes I am and I am weak. The nurse asked did he want something for it? John said no that he didn't need nothing, for pain but he would like something to eat that he was hungry. What would you like to eat asked the nurse? A hamburger' and fries' and a soda. The nurse smiled and said let me ask the doctor and if he says it's ok then we will get you one. John said ok. Tracy looked at John and said welcome back we thought we had lost you. John smiled and said I am not going no, where I got to, much to live for. Where is Muffin asked John? She is at my house she is fine don't worry I will take good care of her said Tracy. Ok John said. The nurse came back in and said that the doctor said that you could have anything that you wanted. Tracy smiled and said one order coming up I will be back shortly. In the mean time Dr. Hampton calls Lt. Smith to let him know that John had woke up and was able to talk. So the lieutenant goes to the hospital to talk to John to see what happen two days before. Lt Smith knocks on the door and goes in John's room. Hello Mr. Martin I am Lt. Smith of the Bellburg "Police I need to talk to you about what happen it won't take long said Lt. Smith. John said sure. Tell me what happen Friday said Lt. Smith. John said I am trying to get into the Import-Export business and I have been looking for investers to help finance the business. I placed ads on some business websites asking for investers who were interested in investing in that type of business. A man that said his name was Perry Hanz emailed me asking for more information about the business. So I sent

him a copy of the business plan that I have. When was this asked Lt. Smith? About three weeks ago said John Ok go" on said Lt. Smith. Then last Tuesday I got an email from Mr. Hanz asking me to call him so I did that Wednesday. What did you talk about asked Lt. Smith? We talked about the business and the money that I need to get into it and he told me that he had forty two million that he wanted to invest and I told him that all I needed was five million. He said yes but that would help the company financially and I asked him how much of the company that he would need for investing that much money and he said forty percent of the company John told Lt. Smith. That is a lot of money to invest in a start up business said the Lt. Smith. Yes sir it is said John. And I asked him why and he said that he liked the business plan and was willing to risk the money John said. I know that you are getting short winded but can you tell me a little more about what happen asked the lieutenant? Ok said John. We agreed to meet this past Friday at my lawyer's office to sign the PPM and contracts his name is Tom Markus also the money was to be transferred Friday as well said John. Ok what happen at your house Lt. Smith asked? I had took a shower and got dressed and went out side to feed muffin my cat when a man in a dark sedan pulled up and got out and asked me if I was John Martin and I told him I was. I asked him his name but he won't tell me. He said that Mr. Hanz wanted his money back I told him I didn't have it that it hadn't been transferred yet. And he said that I was, laying" that he wanted now. I told him to leave and went into the house he came in after me and I got my gun and we started to fight over it and it went off and that is the last thing I remember until I woke up here said John. Ok thank you Mr. Martin that will be all for now said Lt. Smith.

Chapter 2

THE INVESTIGATION
AND TRIAL

As Lt. Smith walked out of John's room he asked Sue to step into the hall. Miss Martin I am going to look into this but it sound's like a scam to me I thank this Mr. Hanz or who ever he is tried to scam Mr. Martin and he tried to kill him self you need to start thanking about getting your brother some help said Lt. Smith. John had no reason to do any thing like that said Sue We will soon found out Lt. Smith said as he walked away. Sue went back into John's room and sit down. John knew that something was wrong. John look at Sue and said you and the lieutenant thank that I tried to kill my self but you are wrong everything happen just the way I said it did. Sue knew that John was telling her the truth but Sue like her mother was a very jealous' women. And she was very jealous of John because John was always able to have better things that her. This was her chance to bring him down. But she didn't stop to thank about what it would do to John. Tracy had got back with John's food and as he was eating Tracy asked Sue what was wrong and Sue said nothing why? John said Sue and Lt. Smith thank that I tried to kill my self. Sue how could you thank a thing like that you know as well as I do John would never do that said Tracy. Sue just looked at them both and said nothing. John ate all the food that Tracy gotten for him. About that time the nurse came in and said how are you feeling? Well you were hungry if you 'keeping eating like that and you will soon be out of here. Do you need anything asked the nurse? Yes I have started to hurt can I have something for it asked John? Sure I will be right back the nurse said. Sue said we are going so you can get some rest if you need me have the nurse's call me ok. Ok John said. As Sue and Tracy was going out the nurse was coming back in. Here you go this is going to make you sleepy I will be back shortly to check on you ok. John smiled and closed his eyes and let the shot take him to dream land. Sue and Tracy left the hospital to go home and as the walked across the parking lot Tracy asked Sue what are you going to do to John? Sue said nothing I will call you later. And she got into her car and left. But Tracy knew that Sue was up to something but she didn't know what.

The next morning Tracy was at the hospital before Sue. She said John we have known each other all our life tell me did you try to kill your self? No John said I have no reason to do that. But Sue and the lieutenant "does and they are going to try to put me away. Tracy said she wouldn't do, nothing like that to you. You don't know my sister like I do she has always been very jealous of me because I had more than she did Sue don't care about the finer things. She just wants to get by but I don't I like having money and a lot of it said John. About that time the doctor came in. How are you feeling this morning Mr. Martin asked Dr. Hampton? I feel ok said John. Good we are going to move you to another room tomorrow said Dr. Hampton. Doctor when can I get out of this bed asked John? You will have to wait until we take that tube out of your side you can sit up but do not get out of that bed said Dr. Hampton Ok John said. Sue came in and said good morning how are you feeling? John said I am going to live Sue said ha ha Tracy smiled and said he be back to his old self in no time. John I will check on you tomorrow said Dr. Hampton. They are going to move John to another room tomorrow said Tracy Good said Sue. I be, glad when I can go home and get out of this place said John. Lt. Smith and his men, was looking into John's story but they wasn't getting any where. They couldn't find the car or the man and the emails, didn't tell them anything. So Lt. Smith said that this man Perry Hanz had coned John out of the money and John tried to kill him self because he was wanting to close the case. So Lt Smith went to the hospital to talk to John again. Sue and Tracy was still their when the lieutenant got there. How are you feeling asked Lt. Smith? Fine said John Great we looked into what you told us and we couldn't found, nothing. We can't find the car or the man nothing said Lt. Smith. I thank you tried to kill your self and made this whole thing up is it Mr. Martin said Lt. Smith. John looked at the lieutenant and said let me make one thing very clear to you and my sister I did not try to kill my self. Now the both of you can thank what ever the hell you want but if I was going to kill my self I would have shot my self in the head not in the chest now get the hell out of here and leave me alone. Dr. Hampton heard what John and the lieutenant was saying and came in and asked' Lt. Smith what he thought he was doing and that all of them had to leave they couldn't up set John that way. As the lieutenant walked out he looked at John and said you are a sick man and I am going to have you put where you can get the help you need. Tracy looked at Sue and Lt. Smith and said you are going to try to put John in a mental hospital aren't you? Sue said yes we are he is sick he needs help. Tracy looked at Sue and said I never thought that you would go this low you two are the ones that need the help not John. Tracy turned and walked away and left Sue and the lieutenant standing there. Sue didn't know it then but she had lost her best friend and brother forever that day. The next day Sue came back to see John but he would not see or talk to her. She called Tracy but she would not to talk to Sue. Tracy kept going to see and talking to John to see how he was feeling. In the mean time the lieutenant done as he said he would and Sue went along with him. It had been three weeks now since John had been shot and Dr. Hampton let John go home. As John and Tracy drove up at Johns house Sue came up and said I am glad that you are home I need to talk to you. John looked at his sister and said leave and I won't say it again. And he turned to go in to the house. Sue said you will soon be in the Bellburg Mental Hospital you are a sick man John. Tracy looked at Sue and said I never would have thought that you would stab John in the back this way I will never have any thing else to do with you now leave and don't come back. Tracy and John went on into the house and John sit down in his chair and Tracy said look who I see and John looked around and saw muffin running next him and as she jumped up in his lap" John smiled and said as he hugged muffin it's good to be home again. Tracy smiled and said yes it is. John and Tracy and muffin spent the afternoon together. Tracy was going to stay with John to help him she would sleep in the guest room. That night Tracy asked John did he need any thing before she went to bed and did he want her to put muffin out side? John said no he was fine and let her stay in side and said goodnight. The next morning John was laying on his back with his eyes closed when he felt muffin standing on his chest he knew the she was looking him in the eye because she wanted him to get up and feed her. John was just laying there as muffin set on his chest and took her paw and hit John on the nose and John open his eyes smiling and said to muffin you want something to eat. And muffin licked him on the nose. So John said ok lets go get something to eat. So John and muffin started into the kitchen and Tracy was up and was fixing breakfast. Good morning how did you sleep asked Traci? I slept like a log said John. Muffin didn't keep you up asked Tracy? No she slept on her side and I slept on mine said John. Muffin looked up as Tracy put her food in her bowl. There you go muffiee smiled Tracy. I want to thank you for taking care of muffin for me said John. I didn't mind I was glad to do it said Tracy. As they were eating the door, bell rang and Tracy went to the door it was Lt. Smith. Tracy asked him what he wanted and he asked to come in. I just came by to drop off this court order. Mr. Martin is to be at the hearing next Monday at 10:00 am he is a sick man and we are going to get him the help he needs said Lt. Smith. You and Sue are the ones that is, sick in the head not me now get out said John. So the lieutenant left and Tracy closed the door. John looked at Tracy and said I am going to loose everything that I have work for. And I want you to see that muffin is took care of. Tracy said I, will. John had to see a Psychiatrist before the hearing and the doctor's name was Dr. Tom Hartman. So he went to see Dr. Hartman and John told him what had happen but he did not believe him. And in the report to the judge he said that he needed to be put in a mental hospital. So that Monday John was there along with Tracy and Sue and Lt. Smith and Dr. Hartman. Lt. Smith told the judge what he had found and the judge talked to Sue and then to Dr. Hartman and he told the judge that John needed to be put in the hospital. So the judge ordered John to be sent to the mental hospital their Bellburg. And the court gave Sue control of everything that John had and all John done was look down.

Chapter 3

THE MENTAL HOSPITAL

As John was leaving the Court Room he looked at his sister and said Sue I knew that you were jealous of me but I never thought that you would go this far. I will never have, nothing else to do with you the longest day I live. Lt. Smith told Sue that John was just mad that he would get over it in a day or two. But Sue knew John meant what he told her. John knew that his life would never be the same. Life as he had known it was over and from now own it would be a living hell. On the way to the hospital John didn't say any thing and as they admitted him he looked at Tracy and said take care of muffin try not to let any thing happen to her because she is all I have left and started next his room. Tracy said ok as she started to cry. Tracy went by John's house and got her things and muffin and went home. John was trying to get use to his new life style but he knew it would not be easy. They bought John some dinner but he couldn't eat it and the nurse came in with his medicine John smiled and said I will take it later and the nurse said ok. But he put it in the toilet. John didn't get much sleep because one of the patients hollered about all night. The next morning John was standing in the door of his room and he was watching another patient a young man that looked in his twenties as he walked over to a lady that was much older than he was and started to bite her. And all the nurses done, was told him to stop. John went back in his room and sit down on the bed. When a very beautiful slender young black nurse came in and said smiling hi I came to change your bandages and John said ok and took off his shirt. John was very muscled up for his age and she liked what she saw. And she said I see that you workout and John said yes I want to stay as healthy as I can for as long as I can I am also into martial art. I am hoping that the doctor will let me bring my weights from home so I can keep on working out. How often do you workout she asked? Three days a week and I watch what I eat and that is going to be hard here said John. Talk to the doctor and she can help you with your diet and by the way my name is Brandi Mitchell. Mine is John Martin glad to meet you said John. If you don't mine me asking how did you get shot asked Brandi? Me and another man, was fighting over my gun and it went off hitting me above the heart and he left me for dead. Everybody thanks I tried to kill my self because it was my gun and my prints on the gun and the GSR all over my hands. But I didn't and the shooter is still out there, said John. Maybe the cops will find him said Brandi. They not looking for him my case is closed said John. Do you need anything asked Brandi? No I am fine thank you said John. If you do need anything let me know said Brandi as she was walking out. Ok John said. John had to fine some peace so he got on his bed and started to meditate and after about two hours Brandi came back in and saw John sitting their and said Mr. Martin are you ok and John said yes I am ok I was meditating that is one of the ways I deal with stress. Oh ok the doctor wants to talk to you said Brandi. As they walked down the hall she asked does that work? And John said it does for me. Can I ask you something asked John? Sure Brandi said. Why do they let that guy bite like he does why don't they do something about it asked John? He has the mind of three year old and we can't do any thing because his family will have the hospital in a big lawsuit he will kick as well watch out for him said Brandi. I will watch out for him but I am going to make one thing very clear if he bites or kicks me I will spank his ass. He has the mine of a child and I will treat him that way but I will not put up with his biting or kicking me said John Watch your back at all times he is very bad about coming up from behind and he does bite hard said Brandi. I will thanks for telling me said John. Sure here we are said Brandi. Hello Mr. Martin I am Dr. Jan Everson I am your doctor come on in and lets talk awhile. So John sat down and looked around the office. Nice office said John. Thank, you, tell me about yourself the things you like to do said Dr. Everson. Will I like to work out do martial arts play on a computer dance travel go out to dinner to name a few and I like the finer things that life has to offer said John. When you say finer things what do you mean asked Dr. Everson? I am very amphibious and very proud man like my father. I like working for my self and taking care of me. I like the multi million dollar homes the big business jets and the life style that goes with it. Doctor I have lost everything I own but there is one thing I will never lose and that is my dignity that no man will rob me of said John. Ok tell me about your family what are they like. Everything was all right until my dad died I was ten at the time. We had an Import-Export business. One day, dad went to the bank to deposit some money when he walked in on a robbery and they shot and killed him he died there in the bank. Sue and I were at school when it, happen. Mom didn't want keep the business so she sold it and after that our life was a nightmare. Mom was the type of person that had to be in control of everything and everybody and she made our life a living hell. Nothing that Sue or I done was right it was always wrong. And the older Sue gets the more like mom she gets. Mom and Sue both have destroyed my love and respect for them. Mom is dead thank God and I will never have nothing else to do with Sue said John. Why she is the only family you have asked Dr. Everson. Doctor my sister is a very jealous and cold, hearted women that only thanks of her self. That is why I am here now. She is selling everything I owned and putting the money in her bank account because the judge gave her control of everything I owned and if you thank I am laying ride by my house and see for your self Sue has always been jealous of me because I have always had more than her. Will you do me a favor asked John? If I can, said Dr. Everson. As you know I like to work out. I have a weight set at home and I was wondering if you would let me bring it here so I can keep on working out and I like to watch what I eat said John. Sure I don't see anything wrong with that said Dr. Everson. Thanks I was hoping that you would let me. I will call Tracy and she can bring it to me. Ok that will be fine. Tell me what happen the day you got shot said Dr. Everson. I got up that morning and took a shower got dressed and went out side to feed muffin my cat she is a long haired Persian and she is black with green eyes at the time we kept her outside said John I would like to see her Persian cats are very beautiful said Dr. Everson. I will tell Tracy to bring her when she brings my weights and you can see her then said John Ok you were tell me how you got shot said Dr. Everson. I had went out side to feed muffin and a man drove up in a blue car and got out he was a very well dressed man and he was wearing gloves like you would wear in the winter and he asked me was I John Martin and I told him I was and I asked him his name and he won't tell me. All he would say is that Mr. Hanz want his money back and I told him that I didn't have it that it hadn't been transferred yet that it was going to be transferred that morning. He said that I was lying that he wanted then. I told him to leave and I went back into the house and he came in after me I got my gun and we started to fight over it and it went off hitting me above the heart and he left me for dead said John. Who is this Mr. Hanz asked Dr Everson? He was the invester that was going to help me to finance the Import-Export business that I was trying get started said John I see said Dr. Everson. Doctor I know that you thank I am lying by that look on your face. But I didn't if I was going to kill my self I would have shot my self in the head not in the chest. The shooter is still out, there and when he finds out that I am not dead he will be back to finish what he started said John. Well that will be all for today Miss Mitchell will take you back to your room said Dr. Everson. As John started out the door he look at the doctor and said I didn't try to kill my self I have to, much to live for. Dr. Everson said Miss Mitchell I want you to keep and eye on Mr. Martin for me and if you see anyone that you don't know asking about him let me know ok. And Brandi said yes doctor. John said I, need to make a phone call. Brandi said ok. So they went by the telephone so John could call Tracy. Hello Tracy said. Hi Tracy its me how you and muffin doing asked John Hi John it is good to hear from you we are doing great she is here with me we are watching TV said Tracy. I don't have much time the doctor said that I could have my weights so I could work out and I was wondering if you would bring them to me asked John? Sure I will be, them to you tomorrow said Tracy. Great and bring muffin too Dr Everson wants to see her and I do too said John Ok see you tomorrow bye said Tracy. Thank you Tracy bye Said John. John looked at Brandi and said thank you and she said you are welcome. And John went in his room and sit down on the bed. He started to smile as he thought about when muffin was a kitten and how they would play with a string or the bell that he had found. There was a knock on the door and it was Brandi and she said there is something I want to ask you. Ok said John as he sit up. I like to work out too and I was wondering if we could work out together asked Brandi? Sure that would be great if the doctor don't care said John. I asked her a just before I came in and she said it was ok. But you have to get well first you can't rush this you are lucky to be alive said Brandi. Not trying to be smart but I am not a, easy man to kill I have a very strong will to live said John. Good keep it that way. Well I am going home I will see you tomorrow. Do you need anything before I go asked Brandi? No I am fine be careful going home theirs a lot of fools on the road said John. I will bye said Brandi. Bye said John as he, laid back down on the bed and he said to his self you lucky jackass. It wasn't very long before they brought John's dinner and it was better than what he had the night before he ate it all and went off to sleep. Dr. Everson couldn't get what John had said off her mind or the look on his face as he left her office. On her way home she went by John's house and there was a For Sale sign in front of it. She wanted to talk to Sue and Lt. Smith so she asked them to come to her office the next day about 3:00 pm and they said they would. The next morning Traci brought John his weights and muffin was with her. A male nurse helped John take the weights to his room, and when they got to John's room Traci put muffin on the floor and she ran and jumped on the bed, and laid, down. John told the nurse thank you and sit down on the bed and hugged muffin. Traci looked at John and said you are looking better you are not as pale as you were. Yes I am stronger than I was when I got here the food is pretty good and everyone has been real nice to me said John. About that time Dr. Everson and Brandi walked in. This must be muffin said Dr. Everson smiling. She is a beautiful cat said Brandi. Yes she is said Dr. Everson. Tracy this is Dr. Everson my doctor and Brandi Mitchell one of the nurses here said John. And they all said hi. Brandi sat down on the bed, side of John and started to play with muffin. She likes to play and likes to be held I got her when she was just a kitten said John. You can tell that she loves you very much, said Dr. Everson. And I love her just as much said John. It was nice meeting you but we have to get back to work bring her back to see us soon ok. Traci said ok I, will. Traci and muffin stayed with John all morning and at noon Traci told John that they had to go so he walked with them to the car and John hugged Traci and muffin goodbye and went back to his room. They brought him his lunch and as he was eating he was thanking about the silly things that muffin had done that morning to make him laugh. John had finished his lunch and sat up in his bed and started to meditate and it had been about two hours when he felt something hit him John looked around and it was the young man that Brandi had told him about he had came in and hit John on the head with his fist. He looked at John and started to laugh and John looked at him and smiled and took him by the arm and as they walked out in the hall John was rubbing his head. And Brandi saw them she ran up to John and asked what happen and John said laughing this young man saw me meditating and thought that something was wrong with me so he was trying to wake me up so he hit me on the head with his fist. Are you all right asked Brandi? Yea I am ok he just caught me off guard he didn't hit me very hard said John. As the male nurses took him back to his room John looked down the hall and saw Sue and Lt. Smith coming next him. He walked up to them and said what the hell do you want? Sue said now is that any way to talk to your" sister. John looked at her and said I won't say what you are because there are ladies here now the both of you get the hell out of here and don't come back. Brandi took John by the arm and said John lets go out side. So John went with Brandi in the yard.

Brandi said John its ok don't let them upset you like this. John looked at Brandi and said if he didn't have that gun on him I would break him in to. Dr. Everson, seen what happen and told Sue and Lt Smith to go with her to her office. So they did and as they sat down Dr. Everson said I thank that it is best that you two stay away from Mr. Martin. No he is my brother said Sue and he is my patient said Dr. Everson and you will do as I say. I saw how much joy you got out of up setting your brother and I won't allow it. She is right he is a sick man we can't up set him like this said Lt Smith. You are wrong lieutenant Mr. Martin in not sick has got as much brains as we have. The reason he is here is because you didn't want to do your job and Miss Martin wanted to be in control of everything because you wanted what he had. No doctor the reason John is here is because the court sent him here. He never would have been here if he hadn't tried to kill him self and if there was nothing wrong with him you would let go home said Sue. Well I am going to do just that said Dr. Everson. You can't do that said Sue The court won't let you said Lt. Smith. That look on your faces tells me everything I need to know and by the way I can and I will discharge him when I get ready to good day folks be careful out there on the road said Dr. Everson. Lt Smith looked at her and said I will stop you from discharging him. She knew then that John was right about his sister that she was, wanting what he had and the reason that Lt Smith wanted him their was because he didn't like John also he wanted to close the case. Lt. Smith went to see the Judge to get a court order from the court to keep the doctor from discharging John. John and Brandi was sitting under a oak tree talking when Brandi said can I ask you something and John said sure you can ask me anything. Why aren't you married you are a fine looking man asked Brandi? Every time I started going with a women my mother and Sue would always find a way to break us up so I gave up. I don't know who you are dating but he is one lucky man said John. Brandi smiled and said thank you. It was getting hot and John said I am going back in side. Me too said Brandi. So John went back to his room and started doing his martial arts. John was a grand master in the martial arts and he enjoyed it very much. As he was doing his work out he started looking at his weights and started to pick them up and as he did Brandi was walking by and saw him and she stop and said don't even thank about. John looked up at her and give' her a devilish smile and said ok and Brandi started laughing and said pointing her finger I mean it and John said ok. She walked a little ways down the hall and turned around and John was talking to one of the other nurses. So Brandi went on down the hall. She was falling in love with John and John was falling in love with her. But they knew that they couldn't let each other know it or any one else. Lt. Smith came and brought a court order to Dr. Everson stopping her from discharging John. Lieutenant why are you so determined to keep Mr. Martin here asked Dr. Everson? Because he is a very sick man and I am going to keep him off the street said Lt. Smith as he was leaving. It had been five weeks since John had been shot and he had, an appointment to see Dr. Mark Hampton the next morning at 10:00 am. So on her way home she went by to see how John was doing. Hi John how is it going asked Dr. Everson? Fine said John Great I just stop by to let you know that you have an a appointment with Dr. Hampton in the morning at ten and Miss Mitchell will be taking you so I am out of here said Dr. Everson. Be careful going home see you tomorrow bye said John. The next morning John was up early taking a shower and was getting dressed when Brandi came in. He had on a pair of black jeans and a white shirt and black cowboy boots. And she said wow you look great. Thank you and so do you I just wish I could wear this all the time said John. Brandi smiled and said thank you. So, John and Brandi went to see Dr. Hampton. They got to his office just before ten and Dr. Hampton told John to come on back. It is good to see you again. You are looking a lot better than you did the last time I saw you said Dr. Hampton. I feel a lot better than I did then said John. Well everything is looking great you have healed good said Dr. Hampton. Can I go back to working out again John asked? Yes you can but don't over do it ok said Hampton. Please tell Brandi that it is ok for me to start working out she won't let me nowhere close my weights said John laughing. John and Dr. Hampton went over to Brandi and Dr. Hampton said everything is fine and he can go back to working out but just don't over do it. By the, way how, much can you pick up asked Dr. Hampton? I bench press 275, said John. Wow be" careful said Dr. Hampton. It was lunch time when they got out of the doctors office so they went by to get something to eat and as they went in John opened the door for Brandi and let her go first and they went over to a table and sat down. They have great food here I think you will like it said Brandi. It has to be with as many people as there is in here said John. About that time a waiter came over and said can I take your order? And Brandi said I, will take the rib eye well done and fries and a salad with French dressing. And I will have the same said John. It wasn't very long before the waiter brought them their lunch. They talked as they ate and when they got ready to go John said this one is on me. Brandi smiled and looked at John and John said it's on me. So John paid for lunch and they started back to the hospital.

Chapter 4

THE SHOOTER

As they left the restaurant John noticed that they, was being followed by a man in a blue car. But he didn't say nothing' to Brandi because he didn't want to upset her. He followed them back to the hospital and as they turned in he parked down the street. As they was walking in Brandi asked John what he was looking at and he said just keep walking I will tell you when we get in side said John. John went to the side door and looked out at the blue car trying to get a good look at who was driving it. Brandi asked John what is wrong? Nothing I hope stay here I am going to get a better look at that blue car and the man that is driving it said John. So John went out the side door and worked his way down the fence so he could get a better look at the man driving the car and it was the man the shot him and he was driving the same car. John wrote down the tag number on the car and went back in side to where Brandi was. Brandi asked who was it? That is the same man that shot me, and that is the same car. Are you sure asked Brandi? Yes I am sure and I got the tag number as well said John. Ok lets go tell Dr. Everson said Brandi. As they started to walk down the hall the man drove off. So they went to Dr. Everson's office because she wanted" to talk to them as soon as they got back. John knocked on the door and Dr. Everson said come in and they both went in side and sit down. Well what did he tell you asked Dr. Everson? He said that everything is fine and that I could start working out again said John. Are you sure that everything is ok I get the feeling that you two are not telling me everything asked Dr. Everson? John and Brandi looked at one another and then John said the man that shot me followed us from the restaurant where we had stopped to get some lunch and he followed us back here to the hospital. What are you sure asked' Dr. Everson? Yes I am sure he was parked down the street and I was able to come up behind him I could see him but he couldn't see me and I got his tag number as well said John. He is not making this up I saw him as well said Brandi. Ok what is the tag number and state asked Dr. Everson? JTHA1245 New York said John. So Dr. Everson called the

Bellburg Police and asked to talk to Lt. Smith. Lieutenant. Dr. Everson on line two for you said one of the officers. Yes doctor what can I help you with said Lt. Smith. Lieutenant Mr. Martin saw the man that shot him here outside the hospital a few minutes ago and Miss Brandi Mitchell one of the nurses saw him as well. Mr. Martin got the tag number and wrote it down this is no joke lieutenant said Dr. Everson. Ok what kind of car was it asked Lt. Smith? It was a blue Lincoln said Dr. Everson. Give me the tag number and I will run it thru the DMV said Lt. Smith. The tag number JTHA1245 New York said Dr. Everson. Ok I will get back in contact with you as soon as I find out anything said Lt. Smith. Dr. Everson looked at John and said the police will find him. He won't do nothing he thanks I am making all this up said John. John was right Lt. Smith laughed and said that nut. And he did nothing. In the mean time the shooter had found his target and he was going to try to make sure that he died this time. As John left Dr. Everson office he told them it is just a small matter of time before I get shot again. John didn't say anything to Brandi as they walked down the hall. He knew that he had to try to keep her and everyone else from getting hurt if he could. As John went into his room he didn't ' saying anything to Brandi. John closed the curtains in his room so no one could see him and sat down on the bed. A short time later Brandi knocked on the door as she came in and she closed it behind her and came and sat down side of John and put her arm around him and said we are going to get thru this together. We are friends and I will stand by you and so will Dr. Everson she knows that you are telling the truth and so do I said Brandi. John hugged Brandi and smiled. Brandi smiled at John and said be ready for a good workout in the morning I will see you at 8:30 ok. John said ok. As Brandi was going out they was bring John his dinner and as he ate he was thanking how he could keep everyone safe. He didn't sleep very well that night because he knew what he had to do. The next morning after breakfast Brandi came in and said I hope that you are ready for a good workout? And John said yes I am let's do' it. For the next two hours John and Brandi worked out and as they were finishing up Dr. Everson came in and asked how was the workout? Great, said John. It was a lot of fun said Brandi. I haven't heard anything from Lt. Smith I want you two to keep your eyes open and keep this between the three of us ok said Dr. Everson. John said and you won't hear anything from that asshole until I get shot again. Will we are going to try to keep that from happening said Dr. Everson. Doctor if it is ok with you I will limit my going outside and when I do I will stay to my self as much as I can that way maybe no one else gets hit. Because it is just a matter of time before he tries it. You know it and so do I and we got to be ready for it said John. Yes I thank that will be the best and be careful the both of you said Dr. Everson. So John started to watch every move that he made. John had been inside for about five days and He told Brandi that he was going out in the yard for a few minutes and so they went out and as they was walking round he was feeling good about himself the doctor was letting him ware his jeans and shirt and boots again and he felt like a man again. It was warm and there was a light wind blowing. As they was' walking next a big oak tree John saw the sun glare off something. And he said Brandi please go inside and get, me something cold to drank. Brandi looked at him. John said I will be ok I be under the oak. So Brandi turned to go back inside when she heard a loud thumb and as she looked back John was laying on the ground bleeding he had been shot. And Brandi scream' John NOOOOOOO as she ran back to him and said don't die. All John could do was look up at her. Brandi screamed call 911 he's been shot help him please. By that time the male nurses had got to John and was trying to slow down the bleeding John had been hit in the chest again and was loosing blood fast. The male nurse looked at John and said hang in there' buddy help is on the way. Dr. Everson came running out to John. The ambulance is on its way she said as she knelt beside him helping the other nurses the best she could. Brandi was standing there crying as one of lady nurses had her arm around her. The nurses had helped the other patients back in side so that the EMT could get to John. By that time the ambulance was there and so was the police. As the EMT was working on John Lt. Smith was talking to Brandi and the others to find out what had happen. Brandi said John asked me to go inside to get him something cold to drank so I did and as I walked off I heard a loud thumb and I turned back around and saw John laying there covered in blood. Did you hear or see anything' asked Lt. Smith? No I am going with him to the hospital said Brandi. Ok that is all for now said Lt. Smith. Did you find out about that car that I called you about asked Dr. Everson? No I didn't I thought Mr. Martin was laying said Lt. Smith. Will he wasn't laying now maybe you and your men will start doing you job and find out who is trying to kill him said Dr. Everson. The EMT was putting John in the ambulance to take him to the hospital. John had lost consciousness as they, was working on him. Brandi went with John to the hospital and they rushed him into surgery. Dr. Everson called Traci and told her what had happen and she came to the hospital to be with her and Brandi. Traci put her arm around Brandi and said' John is a fighter he don't give up. He is going to be all right. He has been here before and has come back and he will do it again. I knew that John wasn't sucidel said Dr. Everson. It wasn't long before Lt. Smith came by to see how John was doing. He looked at Brandi and asked how is he? Brandi said he is still in surgery the doctors hadn't let us know anything yet. We will get the person that did this I promise and also I want to say that I am sorry I didn't believe you and Mr. Martin. That is ok just get the man or women that did this said Brandi. We will said, Lt. Smith. Sue had heard that John had been shot again and came to the hospital and she said what happen. Lt Smith said "your brother was shot by a sniper and that he is still in surgery and that is all I can tell you at this time. As he was leaving Lt. Smith said call me when you find out anything. He handed Brandi a business card with his telephone number on it. Ok I will "said Brandi. What happened at the hospital asked Sue? Why you don't care about him why are, you here anyway asked Traci. Because he is my brother that's why said Sue This isn't the time or the place for you two to get into a fight. If you are going to do that go on the outside said Dr. Everson. Two more hours past and Dr. Hampton came out and said he is in the ICU we have done all we can it is up to John and the Lord now. Can we see him asked Brandi? Ok but only for a few minutes said Dr. Hampton. So they went in to see John and as they were standing there Brandi put her hand in John's and said baby come back to me I need and love you with all my heart and soul don't leave me this way come back to me. And she started crying. Dr. Everson but her arm around Brandi and said John is going to be just fine he is a fighter. He is not one to give up so you don't ether ok. So they went back out into the waiting room. Dr. Hampton went to call Lt. Smith on his cell phone to tell him about John's condition and about the bullet fragment that they took out. Lt. Smith said hello. Dr. Hampton said hello lieutenant this is Dr. Hampton I am calling to let you know that Mr. Martin made it thru surgery and that he in the ICU and we also took out a fragment of a bullet. Lt. Smith said Great maybe that will help us found out who did the shooting. I will be over to get in a few minutes. By the way how is he doing? If he makes it thru the night he will be lucky said Dr. Hampton. Lets hope that he does bye' said Lt Smith. Bye said Dr. Hampton. Lt. Smith went back to the hospital to pick up the bullet fragment so he could take it to ballistics. In the mean time he ran the plate number thru the DMV in New York and found out that the car was registered to a Mr. Mark Henson from New York. So he called a friend of his that worked for the New York Police in Manhattan. Hello Police department can I help you asked the lady? Hello I am Lt. Smith of the Bellburg Police from Bellburg S.C. let me speak to Lt. Tom Marcus please. Just a minute sir said the lady and she looked at Lt. Marcus and said lieutenant Lt. Bill Smith of the Bellburg Police on line two for you. Hello Bill how are you it's been a while. Yea it's been a good while. How is the wife and kids asked Lt. Smith? They are all fine' said Lt. Marcus.

That's great Tom I need a favor said Lt. Smith. Ok name it said Lt. Marcus. We have had a shooting down here and I need all the information that I can get on a man named Mark Henson a car that was registered to him was used in the shooting said Lt Smith. Bill I know Mark Henson very well he's the head of one of the biggest crime families here in New York I will send you everything I have on him said Lt. Marcus. Thanks" maybe there is something in there that will help us get the person that did the shooting said Lt. Smith. Let me know if you need anything else said Lt. Marcus. I will thanks said Lt. Smith bye said Lt. Marcus. Bye said Lt. Smith. As Lt. Smith hung up the telephone he asked himself why would Mark Henson want to kill John Martin? He started to thank about what John had been saying about getting into the Import-Export business. He went over to Sgt. Decker and said get two uniform officers to the hospital now. And Sgt. Decker said yes sir. The two uniform officers met Lt. Smith at the hospital and they went up to the ICU. Lt. Smith asked the nurse what room John was in. And she said 214. Lt. Smith told the two other officers to go to John's room and don't let nobody' in without his ok. And he asked the nurse to get Dr. Hampton. Brandi, Traci, Sue and Dr. Everson wanted to know what was going on. Dr. Hampton came up and asked Lt. Smith what he wanted. Lt. Smith said we have found out that the person that shot Mr. Martin is a professional killer they have tried twice to kill him and we are going to stop them from trying again. He was telling the truth all along and I didn't believe him. Sue said no lieutenant John tried to kill his self and you know it. No Miss Martin he did not try to kill him self. Doctor until we catch the person that shot Mr. Martin only one nurse goes in that room on each shift along with your self and I want their names said Lt. Smith. Traci and I are going in also lieutenant as well as Dr. Everson said Brandi. Ok said Lt Smith. As Sue was leaving four more officers came up to Lt. Smith and he told them what was going on and gave them a list of the people that was to go into where John was. Brandi looked at Lt. Smith and Dr. Hampton and said I am going to stay here with him until this is over I am all he has. I thank that is a good idea that way we can keep an eye on you because you saw the man as well said Lt. Smith. So Dr. Hampton put a bed in John's room for Brandi to sleep on. Dr. Everson went to Brandi's house and got her some clothes to wear and to tell her mother what was going on. Dr. Everson went back to the hospital to take Brandi her clothes and to tell her what her mother said. They went into John's room and sat down on the bed. Brandi smiled and said thank you. Dr. Everson said you are welcome you have a very beautiful little girl she looks just like you. That is what everyone say's Courtney, John and Mom is all I have said Brandi. You love John very much, don't you asked Dr. Everson? Yes I do with all my heart, said Brandi. Well I got a real good feeling that he is going to be all right. John is the type of man the don't give up easy everything is going to be fine I will see you tomorrow ok said Dr. Everson smiling. Brandi's mother brought her something to eat and let the baby see Brandi. As they were leaving she told Brandi to have faith. The nurse, keep a close watch on John thru the night. By morning John was stronger his heart rate was up. Dr. Hampton looked at Brandi and smiled and said he is stronger this morning he has a good chance of making it. And Brandi smiled and said with tears in her eyes he, will we just got to have faith. Faith will take you a long way said Dr. Hampton as he was leaving. Brandi looked at John and said baby come back to me I need you so much don't leave me this way. It had been two days since John had been shot and he was strong enough that Dr. Hampton was going to take him off of life support to see how well he could breathe on his own. Brandi was there along with her mother and Courtney, Traci, Dr. Everson, and Lt. Smith. Dr. Hampton said here we go folks and he turned off the life support. Brandi said come on baby you can do it. John was now breathing on, his own. Brandi and Traci hugged each other as tears of joy ran down their faces. Lt. Smith looked at them and said he is going to be all right and I am looking forward to talking to Mr. Martin. Please let me know when he wakes up.

Dr. Hampton said I 'will. Courtney hugged a round Brandi 's neck and looked at Lt. Smith smiling. Is she always this happy asked Lt. Smith? And Brandi said yes sir 95% of the time she is this way. She is a very beautiful little girl said Lt. Smith as he was leaving. Thank you said Brandi smiling. Lt. Smith's cell phone started to ring as he walked down the hall. It was one of the lady officers they had found the car and the gun was in the trunk. It was a 308 and had a silencer on it. Lt. Smith went to where the car had been found. And they had gotten some finger 'prints out of the car and they got a match. They belonged to Steve Johnson a high paid hit man for the mob. So a, APB went out and law enforcement everywhere was looking for him. It wasn't very long before they found him in a house not far from where the car was found. And as they arrested him Lt. Smith walked up to him and asked why did you shot John Martin? Because I got paid to that's why said Mr. Johnson. Did you shot him both times asked Lt. Smith? Yes I did said, Mr. Johnson. Book him said Lt. Smith. So Lt. Smith went back to the hospital to tell Brandi and the others that they had caught the man that had shot John. Lt. Smith walked up to Brandi with a big smile on his face and said Miss Mitchell we caught the man that shot Mr. Martin and he confess to shooting him both times. That is great said Brandi. We got him at the station now. I am going to find out who hired Mr. Johnson to kill Mr. Martin and why said Lt. Smith. Thank you lieutenant said Brandi. You welcome said Lt. Smith. So Lt. Smith left the hospital to go back the Police station to talk to Steve Johnson about who hired him and why they was trying to kill John. Brandi and the others had walked back to the waiting room and had sit down. Brandi's mother looked at her and said baby he is going to be all right you'll see. I know mama I just don't like seeing him that way. He was always laughing and making everyone smile and now he is in their fighting for his life said Brandi. Traci put her arm around Brandi and said Brandi John has been here before he is going to be ok because he has two of the best reasons in the world to live sitting right here and they are you and

Courtney. And Courtney hugged around her mother and put her head on her shoulder and patted her on the back. Traci said it's getting late I am going to head home call me if you need me ok. Brandi said I 'will. And her mother said we are going too Courtney is getting tired and sleepy. Brandi hugged kissed the baby and her mother and said be' careful going home. And as they were leaving Courtney was waving bye to her mother and Brandi smiled as she waved back at her. Brandi went and got her something to eat and a shower and came back and went to bed. The nurse's was still watching John very close thru the night. The next morning Brandi woke up and went to get her something to eat and came back. It was about noon when Traci came in with them some lunch. And as they were eating their lunch and talking John started to wake up. They put down there food and went to the bed and Brandi put her hand in John's and said that's it come on baby open those big brown eyes for me you can do it. John looked up and smiled at Brandi and said hello beautiful. Brandi smiled at John with tears of joy in her eyes and said hi. Don't cry I will be all right said John and Brandi bent over and kissed him and said ok. Traci smiled went out to the nurse's desk and as she brushed the tears from her eyes she told them that John had woke up. The nurse came in and asked how are you feeling Mr. Martin? And John said I feel ok just weak. Are you in any pain asked the nurse? Not that much said John Do you need something for it asked the nurse? No said John. Will if you do let me know and I will get you something ok said the nurse. Ok said John. Do you need any thing asked the nurse? I would like something to eat I am hungry said John. What do you feel like you can eat asked the nurse as they all smiled. John said I want a burger and fries and a soda. Let me ask the doctor and if he say's its ok then we will get you one ok said the nurse. John said ok. So she went and told the doctor that John had woke up and told him he was, wanting something to eat and Dr. Hampton said to give him what every he feels like he can eat. So the nurse told John what the doctor said. And Traci said I will' be back in a few minutes with your lunch and I will call Dr. Everson and let her know that you have woke up. And, John said ok. So while Traci was going to get John's burger and fries the nurse called Lt. Smith on his cell phone to let him know that John had woke up. Hello said Lt. Smith. Lieutenant I am nurse Baker from the hospital Dr. Hampton wanted me to call you to let you know that Mr. John Martin has woke up said the nurse. Ok great thank you very much, said Lt. Smith. So Lt. Smith went to the hospital to see if he could talk to John. By the time he got there Traci was back with John's food. As John was eating Lt. Smith came in and said hello Mr. Martin I am glad that you are feeling better. Thank you and hello said John. I would like to talk to you a few minutes if you feel like it said Lt. Smith. John said ok. Go ahead and eat your lunch we can talk when you get done. I also want to say that I am sorry about not belicving you. I have talked to Judge Mark Benson and he has signed a court order so that Dr. Everson can discharge you. And until we get the person who master minded this we will keep the officers at your door said Lt. Smith. What did he use to shoot me with a cannon asked John? A small one you were shot with a 308' with a silencer on it that is why no one heard a shot said Lt. Smith. Then I am very blessed to be alive, said John. Yes you are. What happen at the hospital asked Lt. Smith? Brandi and I was walking out in the yard we was going to the big oak side the fence and I saw the sun reflect off something she was looking the other way and didn't see it. So I asked her to go and get me something cold to drank and so she did the next thing I knew I was on the ground with a hold in me and Brandi and the other nurses standing over me I heard one say we got to slow this bleeding down or we will lose him and that's all I remember said John. Can you thank of any thing else at all asked Lt. Smith? John thought a minute and said the only thing that I can thank of is the back' ground check that I done on Perry Hanz but I didn't find any thing but where he had got a few tickets. That's it do you still have it asked Lt. Smith? It was in the files that was on my desk said John. I could be wrong but I am willing to bet that this invester you told me about thanks you know something about him that he don't want nobody to know and so he was going to make sure that you couldn't tell by killing you. And I thank I know who he is said Lt. Smith. Who is trying to kill me asked John? I can't say right now I got to prove it first. Thank you for your help you get some rest now we will talk some more later" said Lt. Smith as he was leaving. The nurse came in to see how much John had been able to eat and she was glad to see that John had been able to eat it all. And she said, good I hope you can keep on eating like this. Is there any thing you need she asked? John said no and smiled. Ok call me if you do she said on her way out. After she went out John had a blank look on his face. Brandi asked John what's wrong? Nothing said John. They will find out who did this said Traci. Are you hurting asked Brandi? John said No. What are you thanking asked Brandi? John looked at them and smiled. John please tell me what you are thanking said Brandi. All John would say is that some things are best left unsaid. John's blood run cold and he knew what he had to do. He was going to do his best to take this person down. John was a martial arts master and he was going to use his skill to avenge his self. He had to find a way to make this man come to him without putting Brandi and the baby and the others in danger. Brandi knew he was up to something but she didn't know what. About that time Dr. Everson came in and said I am glad to see you that you are back with us again you had us worried there for a while. How are you feeling? I am ok just weak said, John. Good I got some papers for you to sign I am going to turn you lose everyone at the hospital said hello and that they will be by to see you said Dr. Everson. Great how is everyone asked John? They are fine they miss you said Dr. Everson. John smiled and said I miss them too. I am sure you do said Dr. Everson laughing. It had been about an hour since Dr. Everson came in and they had been laughing and talking with John. Water was running out of John's eyes. John what is wrong are you in pain asked Brandi? Yes I am said John. How long have you been in pain asked Traci?

Every since I woke up said John. Why haven't you said something asked Brandi? I don't like dope said John. I will go tell the nurse said Traci. Don't do that no more John said Brandi. Ok said John. It wasn't long before the nurse came in with a shot. This will make you sleep she said. We are going so you can get some rest ok said Dr. Everson. I will be back tomorrow 'said Traci. So Traci and Dr. Everson left and Brandi sat down in the chair and as she did she said to her self John Martin what are you up to. It wasn't long before John was a sleep. Lt. Smith had been going over the files that they took from John's desk along with the information that Lt. Marcus had sent to him. He said to his self I could I have been so wrong I should have know that these were pro's. He knew that he needed outside help with this case because he was going to bring the big man down.

Chapter 5

BRING THE BIG MAN DOWN

Lt. Smith went down to the jail to talk to Steve Johnson again. Tell me again why did you shoot Mr. Martin said Lt. Smith? You know he is a dead man and so am I it is just a matter of time said Johnson. Answer the question dam it said Lt. Smith. He was just another job that's all nothing more said Johnson. Lesson to me, I am going to keep you and John Martin alive and you are going to help me do it. For you are going to prison for a very long time Johnson now make it easy on your self and help me to get Mark Henson. Don't say you don't know him because that look on your face say's that you do we know all about you and the work that you do for Henson said Lt. Smith. I will never go to trial I am a dead man they will find a way to get to me said Johnson. You help me and I will keep you alive said Lt. Smith. Ok if I help you get Mark Henson I want all charges against me dropped said Johnson. I can't promise you, nothing but I will talk to the DA and see what he has to say said Lt. Smith. Henson found out that Mr. Martin was' wanting to get into the Import-Export business so he offered to put up forty two million dollars to put him in business and he told him that his name was Perry Hanz because he didn't want him to know who he was. But what Henson had planed to do was to get Martin in business then he was going to have a fatal accident then he was going to take over the business so he could ship guns dope money and women in and out of the country in containers said Johnson. Henson would have a gold mine with this business. Why didn't Henson invest the money asked Lt. Smith? Martin run a back' ground check on Henson and he thought that Martin had found out about his operation so he was going to have him killed and make it look like sucide but Martin pulled thru so Henson told me to make sure I killed him this time or he would kill me. He is one hell of a man said Johnson. Yes he is said Lt. Smith. Lt. Smith knew that as long as Mark Henson was free John would still be in danger and Mark Henson was a very dangerous man. But what Lt. Smith didn't know was that it would be John Martin who would bring down Mark Henson and not the law.

Johnson and Lt. Smith talked a while longer and he went back to his office to check on John so he called Brandi. Hello said Brandi. Hello this is Lt. Smith I was just calling to see how Mr. Martin was. He is doing ok he is a sleep he started hurting and the shot they gave him put him to sleep said Brandi. Ok you try and get some rest too and I will check on him tomorrow bye said Lt. Smith. Ok I will bye said Brandi. Brandi went and got her something to eat and a shower and came back to the hospital her and John slept thru the night. The next morning John woke up before Brandi and as she open her eyes. John said smiling good morning beautiful. Good morning how are you feeling asked Brandi smiling? I feel fine said John. Brandi came over and kissed John as the nurse came in with his breakfast. Try to eat it all said the nurse. John looked at Brandi and said I hope the food is better than the last time. Try it and see and if its not I will go and get you something said Brandi. So John tried to eat his breakfast and it was ok he was able to eat it. The nurse came and got John's tray and said good I am glad you were able to eat it. Do you need anything she asked? No I am fine said John. Ok let me know if you do she said on her way out. John lay back in the bed and looked at the wall and he was thanking about what had happen. He knew that he had to get back what he had if he could. He had to stop Sue from selling his house some how. John looked at Brandi and said princess please call Lt. Smith for me now I got to talk to him it is very important. Ok said Brandi as she dialed her cell phone and handed it to John. Hello Smith here said Lt. Smith. Hello lieutenant this is John Martin I need you to do me a big favor, if you can. If I can what is it asked Lt. Smith? See if you can stop Sue from selling my house and make her give me back the money that was in my bank account. Ok I will have to talk to the Judge I can't promise you anything but I will try. I will see if I can talk to him today ok said Lt. Smith. Great please do what you can because I am not going down with out a fight said John. I will do what I can and I am glad that you are feeling better, said Lt. Smith. Thanks for your help lieutenant bye said John. Any time that is what I am here for bye said Lt. Smith. John looked at Brandi and smiled and said I thank I am going to get my house and money back. Sue isn't going to keep what I got with out a fight. Brandi kissed John and said just don't let this up set you ok and also I want you to know I love you. And I love you with all my heart said John as he hugged Brandi. About that time Dr. Hampton came in to see John. Good morning how are you feeling asked Dr. Hampton? I am fine said John Great lets look you over said Dr. Hampton. When can I start sitting up on the bed asked John? Now if you feel like it but just don't over do it said Dr. Hampton. Ok said John. I will be by tomorrow to see you said Dr. Hampton as he walked out the door. John was setting up on the bed when Traci came in and said well I am glad to see this as she hugged John. I am tried of laying in this bed said John. I know but don't over do it said Traci. How is muffin asked John? She is fine she miss's you as much as you miss her she was asleep when I left said Traci as she sit down in the chair. I am going to ask Dr. Hampton if you can bring her to see me said John. John looked at Traci and asked has Sue sold my house yet? No why asked Traci? I talked to Lt Smith this morning and I ask him to see if the court would make Sue give me back my house and money. I know that she has sold some of my things. But maybe I can get my house and money back said John. Good I hope that you can get them back said Traci. I hope so I want to see her too. About that time Lt. Smith walked in and said I am glad to see that you are sitting up. I have some great news I talk to the Judge and he is going to make your sister give everything back to you. Great thanks said John. Ladies I need to talk to Mr. Martin in private please. So Brandi and Traci went to get something to drank" while Lt. Smith talked to John. Mr. Martin please keep" what I am about to tell you between you and me ok said Lt. Smith. Ok said John. You asked me who was trying to kill you and why the man's name is Mark Henson. He is the head of one of the biggest crime families in this country. He was going to put you in business then have you killed and take over the business. And the reason that he had you shot was because he thought you found out who he was and he was going to make sure you didn't tell anyone about what you found out about him said Lt. Smith. That's just it I didn't found anything, said John. But Henson didn't know that. As long as Henson is free your life is in danger said Lt. Smith. Don't worry about me you keep Brandi and the baby safe and the others safe said John. We are going to keep all of you safe and we are going to get Mr. Henson as well, said Lt. Smith. Please keep me informed said John. " I will said, Lt. Smith as he was leaving. Brandi and Traci came back into John's room and Brandi asked Do you want some lunch? And John said No not now I am not hungry as he looked at the wall. Traci asked what is wrong? Nothing said John What did you and Lt. Smith talk about asked Brandi? I can't tell you said John. You can't or you won't "said Brandi. I can't" said John. Well I am going I have to feed muffin I will see you two later bye said Traci. Bye said John and Brandi. Brandi and John lay down on the bed and John closed his eyes. John knew he had to fine a way to get to Henson before Henson got to him. As John was trying to come up with a way to get to Henson he was being told that John was still alive and that Steve Johnson had been arrested and charged with shooting him by his brother Will Henson. Henson was looking out the window of his mansion and as he turned around he said I hope that you have some good news for me Will said Henson. No I am afraid not Johnson has been arrested and Martin is still alive said Will. Dam I should have killed that fool while had the chance. Ok you go down there and kill Martin and Johnson your self said Henson. Ok said Will. So Will Henson left New York for Bellburg to finish what Johnson had started. It was about 3:00 pm when the court order got to Lt. Smith and he went to Sue's house and knocked on the door and when Sue opened it Lt. Smith said can I come in I need to talk to you it will only take a few minutes. Sure come in can I get you something to drank said Sue. No thanks I have a court order here saying that you have to give John Martin back everything he owned at the time of the shooting. I hope for your sake that you haven't sold anything, said Lt. Smith. I have sold a few things said Sue Well you will have to pay him for the things you sold. And every penny that was in his bank account is to be returned to him said Lt. Smith. You are joking right lieutenant said Sue. No Miss Martin I am not joking you have twenty, four hours and no more to return his property said Lt. Smith. And if I don't said Sue. Then you go to jail good day said Lt. Smith as he was leaving. So Sue called her lawyer and had him to draw up the papers for John to sign where she could give back everything to John. So she went by and picked them up and took them to the hospital. How are you doing asked Sue as she walked in? I am fine said John. Well before you run me off I want to tell you that the court has made me give you back everything you own. As for what I have sold I will pay you for it if that is ok with you said Sue. Sure said John. Here 'is the contracts for you to look over and sign said Sue as she was leaving. Is your address the same asked John? Yes it is said Sue. Then I will mail them to you said John. That's fine said Sue. They was bring in John's dinner when John said baby why don't you go home tonight where you can get some rest I will be alright. Ok call me if you need me said Brandi. I will said, John. So Brandi kissed John and went home for the night. As John was eating his dinner he was thanking. How can I get Henson to come to me? It had been about an hour and the nurse came in and said I hope that you can keep on eating like this where you can get out of here. I am going to try said John. Do you need anything asked the nurse? No I am ok I am just going to watch some TV said John. Ok call me if you do she said as she was leaving. John knew that Henson would send another man to try and finish the job and the bad thing about it was that John didn't know what this guy would look like. He had to find out 'who he was some how. But John knew he was still very weak he had to start to move about to get his strength back he had to be ready this time. John went off to sleep and slept thru most of the night. The next morning John was sitting up on the side of the bed when the nurse came in. Will I am glad you are feeling better said the nurse. I want to get my strength back and I can't do it laying" in this bed said John. But at the same time you can't push your self to hard said the nurse. I know said John. They brought John's breakfast to him. And he had just finished eating when Dr. Hampton and his lawyer came in and asked how are you feeling? John said I am fine I am ready to go home. Not just yet we are going to move you out of ICU this morning and put you up on the next floor and we are going to take that tube out of your side also. Great then I can start getting out of this bed said, John. A little at the time said Dr. Hampton as he was leaving. I am glad that you came in Tom I was about to call you the court has made Sue give back everything I own and she has brought some contracts that I want you to look at before I sign them said John. Ok said Tom. They were getting ready to move John when Brandi came in. What is going on she asked? Brandi this is Tom Markus my lawyer They are moving me up to room 312 on the third floor said John. Brandi smiled and asked how are you feeling? I am fine I want to go home said John. All in good time my darling all in good time said Brandi as she kissed him. How's the baby doing asked John? She is fine she was asleep when I left said Brandi as they went to the elevator. So they put John in room 312 on the third floor. John signed the papers and gave them to his lawyer to mail to Sue. John I am going where I can get these to Sue said Tom as he was leaving. Ok thanks for coming by bye said John. So Brandi called Lt. Smith and Traci to tell them that they moved John out of the ICU and in a private room. As the nurse was leaving she asked John if he need anything. And he said I want to take a bath and shave. I will help him with that said Brandi. Ok said the nurse. So Brandi helped John to take a bath and shave. Feel better now asked Brandi? Yes much better said John as he got out of bed and went to the door. Where are you going asked Brandi? I am going to walk down the hall. I can't get my strength back laying" in this bed said John. So John walked down the hall a little ways and went back to his room. Brandi' said rest some now and you can walk some more later" ok. Ok said John as he got back on the bed. In the mean time Will Henson had gotten to Bellburg and checked into the Bellburg Motel. He called his brother to let him know he was there. Henson started planning how he was going to kill Johnson and John. But first he was going to get him something to eat and a good night's sleep. As John laid there he asked Brandi for her cell phone and the telephone book and so she gave them to him. Who are you going to call asked Brandi? I am going to call Chris Black at the motel a buddy of mine said John. Hello Bellburg Motel can I help you said "Chris. Chris this is John how is it going said John Great how you feeling asked Chris? I am fine just weak they took me out of ICU this morning said John. I went to try to see you but the police won't let know one close you said Chris. Yea they thank someone may try to shot me again. I need for you to do me a favor said John If I can said' Chris. I want you to let me know if anyone from New York checks into the motel said John. Lt. Smith was, wanting to know the same thing. There was a guy that said he was from Chicago checked in last night. I called Lt. Smith and let him know said Chris. What name did he give you asked John? Sam Markus said Chris. What does he look like asked John? He is about six feet tall about 220 Pd black 'hair with a little gray looks to be in his early to mid forties. He has a scar over his left eye said Chris. Ok thanks keep me informed bye said John. You got it buddy bye said Chris. John handed the phone to Brandi as he lay back in the bed. That man has sent another killer down here hasn't he asked Brandi? Yes I thank so. But everything is going to be all right Lt. Smith won't let him get to me said John. I hope not I love you and I don't want to lose you said Brandi. You won't I love you too and we are going to make it thru this. We are going to bring this asshole down that is a promise baby said John. They heard a knock on the door. Come in said Brandi. Hello' you ready to run about five miles with me asked Lt. Smith smiling? No not yet give me a day or two then we will try it ok said John laughing. I here you were walking around earlier I am very glad for you' you have come a long way said Lt. Smith. Yes he has said Brandi. The reason I came by is to tell you that a man from Chicago has check into the motel. And we have a tail on him. He is being watched around the clock. We are trying to found out all we can about this guy said Lt. Smith. Lieutenant we all know why he is here and that is to try and kill Johnson along with me. I want you to keep Brandi and her mother and the baby safe. I can take care of my self said John. We are going to keep all five of you safe. We will have our people watching your house and we have asked the FBI in New York to give us a hand we are going to get these people said Lt. Smith. Lieutenant please" do me a favor bring me a picture of this man ok asked John? I will thank about it. I have to get back to work see you later bye said Lt. Smith. Bye said John and Brandi. They was, bring in John's lunch as the lieutenant was leaving. It was barbecued chicken green beans slaw and ice cream. Brandi took a bite of the chicken and said this is great. John said this is good and they ate it together. I could eat more of this its good said John. By the time Lt. Smith got back to the Police Station two FBI agents was waiting in his office to talk to him. Lieutenant my name is Agent Tom Gibson and this is Agent Ben Sliver we are with the FBI. You call and asked us to help with this case said agent Gibson. Yes thank you for coming so quickly. We are going to need all the help we can get with this one said Lt. Smith. Tell us all you can about this the more information we have the more we can help you said Agent Gibson. Do you know a man named Mark Henson asked Lt. Smith? Yes he runs one of the biggest crime families in this country said Agent Sliver. A man named John Martin that lives here in Bellburg was trying to get into the Import-Export business and was looking for investers to help him finance the business. Henson got in contact with Mr. Martin and told him that he wanted to invest forty two million in the business. But he was using the name Perry Hanz so Mr. Martin didn't know who, he was dealing with. Mr. Martin run, a back, ground check on who he thought was Perry Hanz and he didn't find nothing, and when Henson found out that Mr. Martin had run the back ground check on him. He thought that he had found out who" he was and what he was trying to hide. So he had him shot and we thought Mr. Martin had tried to commit sucide because his prints were the only ones found on the gun and the GSR was on his hands said Lt. Smith. Is he dead asked Agent Gibson? No he is alive like I said we thought he tried to commit sucide so we had him committed to the mental hospital here in Bellburg Henson some how found out that Mr. Martin was alive and sent a man named Steve Johnson to kill him and he all most did. Johnson shot him at the mental hospital but he pulled thru Mr. Martin is recovering in the hospital we have two men at his door round the clock and the only ones that get in are three nurses his doctor and girl friend and a friend of the family said Lt. Smith. Do you have any idea where Johnson is asked Agent Sliver? We have him locked up we found him in a house not very far from here and we have the gun he used to shoot Mr. Martin with said Lt. Smith. Good this will help us a lot said Agent Gibson. We thank that Henson sent another hit man to kill Mr. Martin and Johnson. A man that said he was from Chicago checked in at the Bellburg Motel and he said his name is Sam Markus we got a tail on him said Lt. Smith. His real name is Will Henson he is Mark Henson brother and the best hit man in this country. We have been trying to find him for quite sometime. Mark Henson means business, we have got to watch Will Henson's every move don't let him out of our site. I will call our office and get our team down here said Agent Gibson. So Agent Gibson call's the New York office to get the rest of his team down to Bellburg. So Lt. Smith and the two FBI agents began putting to gather a plan to catch Will Henson while they was waiting for the other agents to arrive from New York. John was working on his own plan. He had a pretty good idea of what Sam Markus looked like and he was going to keep his eyes open. It took only hour and a half for the other agents to fly down to Bellburg. Lt Smith and the other two agents met them at the airport and they checked in at the other motel that was in Bellburg. John what is wrong you haven't had much to say since lunch are, you in pain asked Brandi? No I have just been thanking that's all said John. What is on your mind asked Brandi? I just want to get out of here said John as he set up. It won't be long said Brandi. I got to get out of this bed my back is hurting I am going to walk around the room said John. Ok said Brandi. So John walked around the room and went to the door and looked down the hall. I thank I am going to see if I can run about two miles. You want to come with me asked John laughing? Yea right said Brandi laughing. John stated up the rest of the afternoon walking up and down the hall. Brandi said I am going home and I will be back up here in the morning. Ok I love you be careful going home kiss the baby for me said John. I will and I love you too said Brandi. And they brought John his dinner as Brandi was leaving. She kissed John bye and left. John didn't rest that night he was thanking how he could get Henson with out getting anyone hurt. And he had to come up with something fast. What John didn't know was that Henson would help him. Henson got up the next morning and left the motel and went to the restaurant to get breakfast. He didn't know it but he was being followed. He asked the lady at the restaurant how to get to the hospital and she told him. So he left the restaurant to found the hospital. On his way there he passed the Police Station and he said to him self this is going to be easy. But it won't be as easy as he thought. Because he didn't know that John would become his worst nightmare along with his brother, Mark. Henson went to the hospital to see if he could found out what room John was in. He went to each floor looking for him and when he got to the third floor he saw what he was looking for and as he walked by the room he got the number that was on the door. So he left and went back by the jail to get a look at things and there was a vacant house across from the prison yard and he could see the inmates from it. As he riding around he saw a road that led up to the house. So he went back to the motel to get his things and to check out he would come back into town after dark. So Henson left Bellburg. So Chris Black called Lt. Smith on his cell phone to let him know that Henson had checked out the motel. Hello Smith said Lt. Smith hello lieutenant this is Chris Black at the motel I am just calling to let you know the Sam Markus has checked out said Chris. Ok thanks let us know if he comes back said Lt. Smith. I will bye said Chris. That was Chris Black at the Bellburg Motel Henson just checked out and the boys said the he has left town said Lt. Smith. What is Henson up to asked Agent Gibson? I don't know but we can't let him get away said Agent Sliver. He hasn't done nothing" wrong all we can do is watch, him for now said Lt. Smith. The train was coming as Henson was crossing the train tracks and the officers lost him. So they called Lt. Smith to tell him what happen. Hello Smith here said Lt. Smith. Lieutenant we lost him the train was coming and we couldn't cross the tracks said the officer. Find him I don't care if you have to turn this state up side down but you find him said Lt. Smith Yes sir said the officer. Lt. Smith looked at both agents and said they have lost him and they sit down and shook their head. So Henson went to a town a few miles North of Bellburg. He bought enough food to last him a few days and a sleeping bag and pillow to sleep on. So Henson waited until after midnight to come back in town. Will Henson had been able to get back into Bellburg without the Police knowing it. He was able to hide his car so know one could see it from the road. Also he got things set up in the house so he could kill Johnson the first chance he got. So he called his brother on his cell phone to up date him. Hello said Mark hello big brother I know it's late but I just wanted to let you know that I am going to get Johnson first then I will get Martin. Because it will be easier to get him first I am right a cross from where he is being held said Will. Ok great just get it done and keep me in formed bye said Mark. You got it bye said Will. So Henson sit" back and waited everything was in place. The next day Lt. Smith and Agents Gibson and Sliver went to see John and tell him what happen. Brandi had just got there and gotten out of her car when they pulled up side of her. Hello Miss Mitchell this is Agent's Tom Gibson and Ben Sliver they are with the FBI there are helping me with this case said Lt. Smith. Hello said Brandi smiling Hello said both agents. We need to talk to you and Mr. Martin said Lt. Smith. Ok I am on my way up to see him now said Brandi. So they went with Brandi up to John's room. Hello baby said Brandi as she hugged him. Hello beautiful said John. Good morning Mr. Martin how are you feeling asked Lt. Smith? I feeling great they brought me breakfast a little while ago and Dr. Hampton said I might get to go home by the end of the week said John. That is great news Mr. Martin this is Agent's Tom Gibson and Ben Sliver they are with the FBI they are helping me with your case said Lt. Smith. Hi said John and both agents said hello. As you and Miss Mitchell know we have been following a man named Sam Markus but his real name is Will Henson he is Mark Henson brother we have two men on him but they lost him said Lt. Smith. Then he could be any where said Brandi. Mr. Martin don't worry we will find him said Agent Gibson. Agent Gibson I want a picture of Henson said John. Why asked Agent Gibson? So if we see him we will know who he is and can call you guys said John. In this case I thank that would be a good idea said Lt. Smith. Ok we will get one for you both said Agent Sliver. So they got Brandi and John a picture of Henson. In the mean time Henson was watching the jail and waiting for his chance at Johnson and he won't have to wait for long. They had put Johnson in a room with two other inmates and he had a clear shot and bang. Steve Johnson was dead. Now he would get John Martin. Henson smiled as it started to rain he knew that as hard as it was raining that it would wash away the car tracks. Everything was going as planed he said to him self as he drove off. At the same time the officers was telling Lt. Smith and the FBI that Steve Johnson had been killed. And as they looked around it didn't take them long to find out that Henson was right across the street from them all along. He was right here looking at us said Agent Sliver. He going after Mr. Martin and we got to stop him before he kills him said Agent Gibson. I want four officers and two FBI agents at Miss Mitchell's mother's home now said Lt. Smith. John and Brandi had heard about the shooting on the TV. Lt. Smith called Brandi's mother to tell her what was going on and that Brandi and John was all right. John looked at Brandi and said I want you to go home and stay there until this is over. No I won't leave you said Brandi. Brandi don't argue with me I said go home I don't want you getting hurt or killed you and the baby is all I have." I want to know that you and the baby and your mother is safe". I will be all right now go" leave me your cell phone and call me when you get home I love you bye said John. Ok I love you too bye said Brandi. John called Lt. Smith and told him that he had sent Brandi home and that he wanted to talk to him and the two FBI agents that he might have a way that they could get Henson. Brandi called John and let him know that she was at home safe. Now that John knew that the ones he loved was safe he could come up with a plan to get Henson to come to him and to get Lt. Smith and the FBI to go along with it. So Lt. Smith and Agents Sliver and Gibson went to talk to John. Lt. Smith knocked on the door as they came in and John said hello thank you for coming. I thank I have a way that we can get Henson. How asked Agent Gibson? We all know that Henson is watching this hospital. So you get the doctor to discharge me where I can go home because I am out of danger I can walk a round I am weak but ok said John. Go on said Lt. Smith. We will let Henson see me leave and let him follow us home. Agent Sliver will be with me at home. And the rest of you stay for enough away that he won't get suspicious of anything and let him come to the house after me. Then you close in and get him said John. That is putting your life in to much danger no said Agent Sliver. I will have one or two of your people with me I will be all right. Have some faith in your men. And this way you can get to him before he gets to me and this maybe the only chance you have to get Henson said John. I hate to say it but he's right said Lt. Smith. You are a brave man Mr. Martin said Agent Sliver. I just doing what I got to do to get this asshole before he gets me". Gentleman, don't let Brandi know what we are going to do I don't want her to know anything until this is all over ok said John. Ok, also I will let every one know what we are going to do said Lt. Smith. So while Lt. Smith was informing the others. Agent Gibson got Dr. Hampton to let John go home the next day. As John had said Henson was watching the hospital and he saw John getting in the car with Agent Sliver but he didn't have a clear shot. So he followed them to John's house. Henson left his car where no one could see it from the road. He came thru the woods to the back of John's house as John and Agent Sliver was going inside. Henson decided to wait until it was dark to kill John so he sit" back and waited. John sit down in his chair and started thanking that his plan to get Henson was working. John knew that Henson was close by he could sense him. And John knew it wouldn't be very long before he would be fighting Henson for his life. But he wanted it that way. "To have a one on one with Henson for he was going to beat the hell out of him". Do you need anything Mr. Martin asked Agent Sliver? No I am fine thank you said John. John was not going to make it easy for Henson. He would have to come in side to get him and that is just what John planed. John and Agent Sliver, was watching TV when they heard something out side. Stay here said Agent Sliver as he pull out his gun and went to the window and looked out but he didn't see any thing so he went to the kitchen door and Henson was their waiting and shot him thru the door. And as Agent Sliver fell back Henson came thru the door. By that time John had got up and was waiting for him. John thought that Agent Sliver was dead. As Henson came closer John hit him with everything he had and he went down and the gun fell on the floor. John jumped on top of Henson and started to beat him in the face and it took

only two punch's to knock him out by that time Lt. Smith and
Agent Gibson and the others had got there. Agent Sliver is shot
said John. A, ambulance is on the way said Lt. Smith. Are you
all right asked Agent Gibson? Yea I am ok now I am going to get
my ass kicked by Brandi laugh John. We won't let her beat you
up to bad said Lt. Smith laughing. Now we can bring down
Mark Henson along with the rest of his gang said John. Yes we
will but you won't, said Agent Gibson. Your life has been placed
in danger to many times now said Lt. Smith. An as long as
Henson is out there my life will stay in danger along with Brandi,
Courtney, and Brandi's Mother and Henson is not getting to
them I mean it said John. He won't said, Agent Gibson. As they
led Will Henson out the door he looked at John and said you are
a dead man. As you and your brother know by now I am not an
easy man to kill and I will get Mark Henson just like I got you.
Now get this asshole out of my house said John. So they took
Will Henson in to book him. Now I got to go and buy a door
said John. We have got it where it will shut said Lt. Smith. Will
you let one of you men take me to Brandi asked John? Sure I will
take you said Lt. Smith. Can we stay here tonight I sure would
like to sleep in my own bed if I could asked, John? I don't see
why not just don't go into the kitchen until we say you can said
Lt. Smith. Ok said John. The ambulance was on its way to the
hospital with Agent Sliver. Lt. Smith took John to where Brandi
was and as they came into the house she hugged around John
and he hugged her back. I thought you were in the hospital said
Brandi. No Dr. Hampton released me so I could help Lt. Smith
get Henson and we got him Agent Sliver got shot but we are
hoping that he will be ok said John. John Martin you could have
been killed what was, you thanking said Brandi. I was thanking,
of " you and the baby and your Mother trying to keep you three
from getting hurt. Because you three and Muffin is all I have. I
love you princess and I love Courtney with all my heart and I
didn't want you to get hurt or killed don't be mad said John. I
am not mad I just don't want you to get hurt ether because we

love you too said Brandi as she kissed John. Well she didn't beat you to bad Mr. Martin laugh Lt. Smith. No not as bad as I thought said John laughing. Well I am going to the hospital to check on Agent Sliver said Lt. Smith. Let us know how he is doing said Brandi. I will Lt. Smith said as he was leaving. Well I am going back home and I was wondering if you and the baby would like to come with me asked John? Yes we would let me get us something to wear said Brandi. John went over to Courtney and started to play with her. And in no time he had her laughing out loud. And Brandi got them some clothes and came back in the room and what she saw made tears of joy run down her face. Ok I am ready said Brandi. Come on darling said John as he picked her up. Careful John don't, hurt your self said Brandi. I won't, said John as they went out to the car. The baby was still laughing as hugged around John. Brandi opened the car door and John put Courtney in her car seat and Brandi's Mother hugged all three and said call me when you get there. We will said, John. So they went to John's house and on the way they stopped at a, all night market and got them some food so they would have something to eat. By the time they got there the Police had gotten all they needed out of the kitchen and the officer helped John fix the door where it would close. Brandi called her mother to let her know that they were there. About that time they hear a car drive up and Brandi looked out and it was Traci and Muffin. So she opened the door and Muffin ran to John and jumped up in his lap, and, licked him on the nose as he hugged her. Come on in Traci it is good to see you have, seat said Brandi smiling. I can't stay long Lt. Smith called me and told me you were home and I knew that you would be wanting Muffin at home with you so I brought her home said Traci. Yea I was going to call you and ask you to bring her home thanks Traci said John. Sure I was glad to I am going to miss her said Traci. Muffin was on one side and Courtney was on the other side of John's lap. Courtney and Muffin played with each other while John Brandi and Traci talked. Well I got to go where you two can get to bed said Traci as she was leaving. Thanks again for bring Muffin home said John You are welcome bye said Traci Bye said John and Brandi as she closed the door. Courtney had fallen a sleep in John's arms and Brandi took her and laid her on the bed and put a pillow behind her to keep her from falling off the bed. And Muffin followed Brandi and had laid "down on the bed, side of Courtney and had put her paw on her hand and went to sleep. Brandi went back out to where John was and sat down side of him and said our two babies are a sleep now I want you to spend some time with me as she kissed him. Lets finish this in the next room said John. Ok said Brandi. So they went to bed and for the next two hours they made love and they talked for a while and then Brandi fell a sleep in John's arms. And as John was laying their holding Brandi in his arms he was thanking. For the first time in my life I am truly happy and I am not going to let Mark Henson or no one else take it from me. So John went on off to sleep a very happy man that night. The next morning Brandi and John had woke up and was "laying there, talking when Muffin came in and jumped up on the bed and went up to them and lick them on the nose. Good morning Muffin said John as he hugged her. And Brandi went to see if the baby was a wake and she was still a sleep. So Brandi went and lay back down side of John and they played with Muffin for a while and she wanted something to eat. So while John was feeding Muffin Brandi went to get Courtney for she had woke up and was playing with her toes. So Brandi put a dry diaper on her and picked her up and gave her a big hug and kiss and they went in where John and Muffin was. And John asked smiling how is my little princess this morning? She put her little arms out smiling for John to take her. So he did and Brandi started to fix breakfast for them. The telephone started to ring it was Lt. Smith. Hello said John. Hello Mr. Martin Smith here I am just call to let you know that Agent Sliver is going to be fine he wasn't hurt as bad as we thought said Lt. Smith. That is great thanks for letting us know I will tell Brandi we will be up to see him later today said John. Ok I will tell him. His wife flew in last night to be with him he is in room 415, said Lt. Smith. Have you got any thing out of Henson asked John? No his lawyer won't let him say nothing well I just wanted to let you know about Agent Sliver. Hug the baby for me ok bye said Lt. Smith. I will bye said John. That was Lt. Smith he said that Agent Sliver is going to be all right and is going to make a full recovery said John. That's great said Brandi. Mark Henson didn't sleep to good the night before as he was trying to thank of away to get his brother out of jail and kill John at the same time. So he started to come up with a plan. He would come down to Bellburg and kidnap a child and then he would tell the police to release Will or he would kill the child and that would get John Martin out in the open as well and he was going to do this him self thought Henson. So he told his men what he was going to do and it wasn't very long before they were on their way to Bellburg S.C. But what Mark Henson didn't know was that he wouldn't leave Bellburg " a live. John put the baby in her high chair and sat down at the table and started to eat his breakfast and he said this is real food this great. I was hoping that you would like my cooking said Brandi smiling. If I keep eating like this I will be fat as a pig soon said John. No you won't I will put you on a diet and make you work out. I am not living with a fat man said Brandi laughing. Ok we will see said John laughing. So they ate breakfast and went to the hospital to see Agent Sliver. They knocked on the door as they went in. Hi we thought we would come by and see how you were feeling said Brandi. I am feeling a lot better than I was last night. Good said Brandi. John looked at Agent Sliver and said smiling some men will do almost anything to get to talk with a beautiful nurse. I like to talk to the women but I wouldn't go this far said Agent Sliver smiling. All right Ben Sliver said Mrs. Sliver smiling. Jane I would like for you to meet Miss Brandi Mitchell her little girl Courtney and Mr. John Martin and this is my wife Jane said Agent Sliver. And everyone said hi. I didn't know how bad you were hit I am glad that you are going to be ok said John. Thank you I will be glad to go home said Agent Sliver. It won't be long they will take very good care of you here we have some of the best doctors and nurses in this country right here in Bellbure said Brandi. Yes I am living proof of that said John. You have a little angel there, said Mrs. Sliver Thank You said Brandi Well we are going so you can get some rest we hope you enjoy the fruit said John. I will thanks for coming by said Agent Sliver. Bye said Mrs. Sliver. So they left and went back home so John could get some rest also. In the mean time Lt. Smith and Agent Gibson was getting no where" with Will Henson. He wouldn't talk to them so they put him back in the cell. Mark Henson and his gang had gotten to Bellburg and was in old house that they had found and Henson told two of the men to find a child about nine or ten and two kidnap him or her and bring him or her to him unharmed. It wasn't long before they found what they was, looking for. A very beautiful little girl she was nine. So they took her to Henson. Darling we are not going to hurt you as long as you do as you are told ok said Henson. Yes sir she said. What is your name asked Henson? Sally Rogers said Sally. Are you hungry Sally asked Henson? No sir said Sally. When you do let us know and we will get you something ok said Henson. Yes sir said Sally. Put her in the other room and watch her said Henson. So they put her in a room that didn't have no widows and one door. Henson had a battery operated TV. He knew that when Sally didn't come home after school that her Mother and Father would be looking for her and then he would let them and the police know that he had her. And so they started to look for Sally and Henson let them know that he had her and that she wouldn't be harmed if they let him have his brother and John Martin. John and Brandi had been watching the news when Lt. Smith and Agent Gibson knocked on their door. May we come in asked Agent Gibson? Sure come in said John. I suppose you have heard the news asked Lt. Smith? Yes what are we going to do asked John? John Martin what do you mean we said Brandi. Henson wants me I don't thank he will hurt this little girl if we do as he says and we can't take a chance with her life said John. You are right but we can't put yours in danger ether said Lt. Smith. He is right John said Brandi. There is no, other way you know it as well as I do. There is only one way to end this and that is for me to kill Henson and the men that he has with him. John what are you saying said Brandi. It is the only way Brandi said John. He's right Miss Mitchell said Agent Gibson. Where are they holding her asked John? In the old house on Epps Rd. said Lt. Smith. Ok that house has a hill in front and on the side I will be able to see them but they won't see me. If you will get me what I need I will end this and bring Sally back to her Mother and Father alive and well said John Tell us what you need said Agent Gibson. I need the same thing that Steve Johnson used "on me and a 9MM both with a silencer and I want four clips for the 9MM and a cell phone said John. So Lt. Smith called and got what John wanted. It will be there when we get there let's go said Lt. Smith. So John and Brandi went with them to where Sally's Mother and Father was" and Lt. Smith told them what they had planned to do. I am not going to tell you not to worry but I will say don't worry too much I will have Sally back home safely to you before long I promise. And I don't make a promise that I can't keep said John. John you come back to us the same way you are leaving don't be a hero I love you said Brandi crying. Don't cry princess I will be ok and I love you both said John as he hugged Brandi and kissed her and the baby good bye. Be careful said Lt. Smith. I will and I call you when I have her said John. So John got into the car and left. That is one hell of a man said Lt. Smith. Yes he is said Brandi. He is going to be ok Miss Mitchell said Agent Gibson. As John was driving along he was thanking everything was working out as he had hoped. Now he was going to get the man that was trying to kill him. It wasn't long before John got to Epps Rd. and he stopped his car and got out and put the 9MM on his side along with the other clips and the silencer in his pocket. He put the 308 a cross his shoulder and walked down the road a little ways and then he started to climb up the hill so he could have a clear view of the house with out them see him. It was a full moon that night so John got where the moon was behind him so it wouldn't reflect off the scope and give him away. He had everything set and there was, four men out side and they was one on each side of the house. So John aimed at the first and bang he was dead and then number two and then number three and then number four. John put down the rifle and started down the hill and he came up from the back of the house. For he knew that it wouldn't be very long before Henson would miss his men so he had to move fast. So he took out the 9MM and put the silencer on it and started around the house to see if he could see Henson and he was a sleep in the living room so John was able to sneak up on him an put the gun to back of his head and said wake up Mr. Henson we meet at last. Don't even thank about going for that gun because I can't miss at this range. Now take it out nice and slow with two fingers and keep the other hand where I can see it. I just killed four the men that was with you and I will kill you just as quick if you make the wrong move. Who are you asked Henson? I am the man you have been trying to kill. Where is Sally asked John? She is in their said Henson. John went to the door and opened it and asked Sally you in there? Yes sir said Sally. Come on out I won't hurt you I am here to take you back to your Mother and Father said John. So Sally came out to where John was. Are you all right did these men hurt you asked John? No sir they didn't hurt me said Sally. Henson went for his gun and John shot him hitting him in the heart and he fell over dead and John hugged around Sally and said it is over I am going to take you home. So John took out the cell phone and call Lt. Smith. Hello Smith here said Lt. Smith. Hello lieutenant it is me" John I got her and she is find just scared and I am fine and tell Brandi I love her and is coming home with the little one and we are going to need the coroner as well Henson and his men are dead said John. He has her and they are both fine, said Lt. Smith. So John took Sally back to her Mom and Dad and as they drove up in the drive, way Brandi and Mr. And Mrs. Rogers came running out to meet them. And as they hugged around their little girl Brandi hugged around John. Mr. Rogers said we will" never be able to thank you enough for what you have done. Knowing that she is safe and back here with her Mom and Dad is, all the thanks I need said John. And Sally went over to John and hugged around him and looked up and said thank you Mr. Martin. And John said you welcome darling. Brandi looked at John and said lets go home and get some sleep it has been a long night. Yes it has said John. So Brandi puts Courtney in her seat and they say goodbye to each other. And Sally and her Mom and Dad wave as John and Brandi drive off.

Chapter 6
THE MULTIBILLIONARE

On there, way home John didn't say very much to Brandi for he was thanking about what he had done. He had never kill a man before and it wasn't a very good feeling and he knew that it would take some time to for get what happen. He was thankful that it was all over now and that everyone was safe once more and that they could get on with their life. John drove up in the driveway and they got out and as Brandi unlocked the door John took their little sleeping angel out of her seat and went in the house and put her down on the bed and Muffin jumped up on the bed and laid down side of her. You want me to cook you some breakfast asked Brandi? No I just want a sandwich we both have been up all night and I know that you are tried. So fix us a sandwich and let's get some sleep said John. Ok baby order coming up smiled Brandi as she hugged John. So Brandi fixed them a sandwich and they went to bed. Brandi had backed up to John and he said I love you princess. I love you too said Brandi. So John and Brandi and Courtney slept most of the morning. Brandi was still a sleep so John got up to see if Courtney was a wake and she was still sleeping. So John went and laid back down side of Brandi and Muffin came in and jumped up on the bed next to John and laid' down. John was wondering why Mark Henson was' wanting him dead. He was going to talk to Will and see if he would tell him why. So John played with Muffin for a few minutes and then they got up and went into the kitchen and John feed Muffin and took out some chicken for lunch and he went back in to check on the baby and she was a wake so John put a dry diaper on her and took her in the kitchen to feed her. And as he was Brandi came in. Good afternoon said John. What time is it asked Brandi? 1:30 pm said John Why" didn't you wake me up I would have fixed you two something eat said Brandi. I knew that you were give" out so I let you sleep said John. How long have you two been up asked Brandi? The baby has been a wake about forty' five minutes and I been up about an hour I want to get another door to day said John. Ok said Brandi. I am all so going to talk to Will Henson I want to know why his brother was trying so hard to kill me said John. So they ate lunch and took a shower and went to get a kitchen door and on the way back they stopped by the jail so John could talk to Henson. Henson you got a visitor come' with me said the officer. Who is it Henson asked? The man you tried to kill said the officer. So Henson went to see John. Hello Mr. Henson my name is John Martin I see that they are treating you very well said John. Yes they are what do you want asked Henson? I just want to know why your brother wanted me kill. I never did nothing' to him. Why was he trying to kill me asked John? It was because you run the back ground check on Mark and found out about us so he was going to shut you up so you couldn't tell the police what you knew said Henson. Well I got news for you Mr. Henson the only thing I found was where he had two tickets for parking that is all I found said John. What you are laying said Henson. No I am not laying those two parking tickets got your brother killed and you are going to jail for a long time let it end here. If your brother had left me alone everything would have been fine. There is no reason for any one else to die. I just want to live in peace said John. You are right too many people has die over this. Go in peace Mr. Martin you have nothing more to fear from me or our people said Henson. Thank you said John. And he went back out to where Brandi and they baby was Lt. Smith had walked up and was talking to them. What did he say asked Brandi? He told me that the reason Mark Henson wanted me dead was they thought that I had found out about what their business was. And he was going to shut me up to keep me from telling anyone said John. So all, of this killing was about the back, ground check you run asked Lt. Smith? Yes lieutenant that was what it was all about said John. Lets go home you have a door to put up said Brandi smiling. Be careful and don't hurt your self said Lt. Smith. I will said, John. So they left and went home and John and his neighbor put up the kitchen door. John went and sat down by Brandi and asked what's wrong princess? I wish that I didn't have to go back to work at the hospital said Brandi. You don't you can quite if you want to I have enough money coming in that you don't have to work if you don't want to said John. So Brandi was able to quit her job at the hospital and she was glad to be able to do so. Now she was a full time Mom and was a very happy one. It had been six weeks since John had been shot and he had started to work out again and had gotten muscled up like he was before and he was just as good now at martial art as he was then. John and Brandi was" very happy with each other and got along great. And then came the day that would change" their life forever. They were watching Muffin and Courtney play on the floor when they heard a knock on the door. And John went to the door and opened it and said can I help you. Are you John Martin asked the man? Yes I am who are you asked John? My name is John Samson I represent Mr. John Clark may I come in asked Mr. Samson? Yes come on in what is this all about have a seat said John What a beautiful little girl said Mr. Samson. Thank you said Brandi. Mr. Samson this is my girl friend Brandi Mitchell said John Hi nice to meet you Miss Mitchell said Mr. Samson. Like wise can I get you anything asked Brandi? No thanks said Mr. Samson. Mr. Martin I won't take much of your time. Like I said I represent Mr. John Clark Mr. Clark owns Clark Import-Exports and he has cancer and has six weeks to live. And he wants to give you control of the company while he is still able to do so and he would like for you to fly down on his jet to meet with him said Mr. Samson. Why would Mr. Clark be willing to leave his company to me when I have never meet the man asked John? He has no family he never has got married and he wants to turn the company over to you before he dies. Mr. Clark knew your father they were good friends and he knows that you want a Import-Export company of your own so he is giving you his said Mr. Samson. How much does the company owe the bank and where are they based out of asked John? The company is in two billion in debt and is worth Forty Billion the company does over a Trillion in business a year and they are based out of San Juan, Puerto Rico said Mr. Samson. Wow ok that is a hell of a company said John. Yes it is said Mr. Samson. Well let me thank about it and I will get back in touch with you in a few days said John. Ok here is my card let me know what you decide to do and thank you for your time said Mr. Samson as he was leaving. I will thank you said John. What are you going to do asked Brandi? I am going to find out all I can about these two men especially Mr. John Clark said John as he picked up the telephone to call Lt. Smith. Hello Smith here said Lt. Smith. Hello lieutenant this is John Martin. How you doing asked John? I am doing "good. How about all of you asked Lt. Smith? We doing great I need a favor if you will. We just had a visit from a man that says his name was John Samson. He is a lawyer from San Juan, Puerto Rico. He said that he was representing Mr. John Clark and that he owns Clark Import-Exports. And that Mr. Clark "was wanting to give me control of the company and it is worth Forty Billion. If you will fine out all you can about Mr. Clark because nobody just gives up a Forty Billion dollar company said John. You are right about that. Did he leave a card with his name and number on it asked Lt. Smith? Yes he did said John. Are you going to be home this evening if so I will run by and get it on the way home ask Lt. Smith? Yes we will be here all evening said John. Ok I will pick it up then and I will find out all I can. We don't want another Mark Henson on our hands said Lt. Smith. You got that right we will see you then bye said John. Bye said Lt. Smith. Lt. Smith is coming by on his way home to pick up this card. He is going to find out who John Clark is said John. Good said Brandi. So early that evening Lt. Smith drives up in front of John's house and goes to the door and knocks. Brandi goes to the door and it is Lt. Smith. Hi come in thanks for coming by said Brandi. You welcome hey darling she is as beautiful as ever said Lt. Smith. Thank you John has her spoiled said Brandi as she gave the card to Lt. Smith. Courtney was in John's lap smiling at the lieutenant. You are only little once said John laughing. After you called me this afternoon I made some phone calls and I have been able to find out that Mr. John Clark is an honest business man" also he is one of the richest men in this world. He is the man that bought your father's business after he was killed. And the man that came to see you earlier is, his lawyer said Lt. Smith. Now I can get back what my Mother took from me so long ago said John. Well I better be, going bye pretty girl said Lt. Smith. Courtney just smiled at the lieutenant. Thank you for your help said John. You welcome that is what I am here for good night said Lt. Smith. Good night and thanks said Brandi. Well baby I am going to get my fathers business back said John. I have always like good looking' men that was super rich said Brandi as she hugged around John laughing. Is that right said John' laughing. Yes sir said Brandi. This will mean a better life for all three of us and I can give you and Courtney the best of everything said John. And you will be getting that big business jet like you have been, wanting said Brandi. Yes it will be a very big change for all of us. Lets go out for dinner said John. Ok I need to take a shower and give the baby a bath and get dressed said Brandi. Lets take your Mom with us too I will call her and let her know said John. Ok said Brandi. So while Brandi and Courtney took a bath John call Brandi's Mother and told her they were going out to dinner and they wanted her to go with them and they would pick her up in a little while. While Brandi and Courtney got dressed John took a shower and got dressed and they went by and got Brandi's Mother. As they rode along Brandi said Mom John is going to take control of a multibillion dollar" company. Yea right and I am, Johnnie Carson said Mrs. Mitchell. Brandi is telling you the truth. Mr. John Clark brought my Father's company when he died. Now he has cancer and don't have very long to live and he is giving me control of the company while he still can said John. That is great. I am happy for the both of you said Mrs. Mitchell. We are going to fly down to talk to him John is going to call him in the morning to make all the arrangements. That is if John will let us go with him said Brandi. I will thank about it said John laughing. If you don't I won't give you no more loving said Brandi smiling. John speaking as a women" I would let her go if I were you said Mrs. Mitchell laughing. Ok you talked me into it said John. That works every time said Brandi as she reached over and kissed John on his face. So they went in the restaurant and had a good meal and a fun filled evening. It was get late and Courtney was getting sleepy and on the way home she fell a sleep in her seat. They took Brandi's Mother back to her house and said good night. And went on home and when they got their Brandi opened the door while John got the baby and they went in the house and John put Courtney in her bed and John and Brandi undressed and went to bed. The next morning John call's Mr. Samson at the motel. Hello said Mr. Samson. Hello Mr. Samson this is John Martin and I have decided to take Mr. Clark up on his offer said John. Good Mr. Clark will be very happy I will call him and let him know. When can you leave ask Mr. Samson? What about in the morning asked John? Ok that is great I will arrange for a limousine to pick you up and take you to the airport where your jet will be waiting in the morning said Mr. Samson. Brandi and the baby will be flying down with me as well said John. Ok that will be fine. What time would you like to leave asked Mr. Samson? About 9:00 am will be fine said John. All right I will make all of the arrangements and we will be looking forward to seeing you folks in the morning have a good day bye said Mr. Samson. Bye said John and hung up. Brandi hugged around John and kissed him and said I am very proud of you. You have gone through a living hell and now your dreams are becoming reality. Yes at last we can have the finer things that this life has to offer. From now on it will be only the best for you and Courtney said John as he hugged Brandi back. So they ate breakfast and while Brandi was packing their clothes and getting thing ready for their trip John calls Dr. Everson to tell her. Hello Bellburg Mental Hospital said the nurse. Yes I would like to talk to Dr. Jan Everson please said John. May I ask who is calling please asked the nurse? John Martin said John. Just a minute I will tell her you are on the line said the nurse. Hello John it is great to hear from you. How are things going asked Dr. Everson? There are doing great Brandi and Courtney are" doing fine and as for me I fine. I know you that you are busy and I won't keep long. But do you remember when I told you that I like the finer things in life said John. Yes, said Dr. Everson. Well it is becoming reality I am take control of a multibillion dollar" Import-Export Company. We are flying down in the morning to sign the contracts and Brandi and the baby is going with me said John. That is great I am so happy for you. It was a long time coming and you went thru hell but you didn't give up. I am very proud of you John I really am said Dr. Everson. Thank you well I will let you go bye said John. Bye and good luck and tell Brandi hello for me said Dr. Everson. I will bye said John. How is she doing asked Brandi? She is fine and she said to tell you hello and she said good luck said John. So John and Brandi spent the rest of the day getting ready to go to Puerto Rico. He called and told Traci and asked her to feed Muffin for him and she said she would. John and Brandi didn't get to much sleep that night for they were to excited" about the trip to sleep. John had his mine on how he was going to run the company and hoped that everything would go smooth for him. They were up early and got dressed and eat breakfast. John feed Muffin. About 8:15 the limousine came up and as they were leaving John hugged Muffin and told her to be a good girl. So they went to the airport where the big business jet was waiting along with Mr. Samson. Good morning it is good to see you Miss Mitchell Mr. Martin said Mr. Samson as he was shaking hands with them. Good morning sir said John. Miss Mitchell Mr. Martin I would like for you to meet our Captain Miss Kelly Young and her First Officer Justin Marshall and this is Miss Brandi Mitchell and her beautiful little girl Courtney and Mr. John Martin your new boss said Mr. Samson. Brandi and John both said hello and nice to meet you as they shook hands. Courtney didn't know who these people were and she didn't understand what was going on but she was smiling anyway. Its nice to meet you said Brandi and John. So while there luggage was being loaded Brandi Courtney John and Mr. Samson went and got on the jet. I like this said John as they looked over the jet. It has a bedroom in the back of the plane so if you want to" lay down you can, said Mr. Samson. This is like the one you told me about said Brandi. Yes is what I been wanting said John. Excuse me sir we have your luggage loaded we are ready to take off when you are said Miss Young. Ok lets put this big bird in the air said John. Yes sir said Miss Young. It wasn't but a few minutes and the big jet was in the air and they was" on their way. It took about four hours to fly down. Mr. Martin we will be landing in about ten minutes said Miss Young. Ok thank you said John. They felt the big jet touch the runway and as it stopped a big limousine pulled up side of it and a tall well dressed man got out and stood up. Brandi Courtney John and Mr. Samson walked off the big jet. Mr. John Clark this is Miss Brandi Mitchell her daughter Courtney and her boy friend Mr. John Martin said Mr. Samson. Hello I am glad to meet you Miss Mitchell and your beautiful little girl said Mr. Clark. We are glad to meet you and thank you said Brandi. It has been a long time since I saw you. How you been asked Mr. Clark? It is good to meet you and I am doing great said John. How was your flight down asked Mr. Clark? It was great said John. So they left the airport and started to Mr. Clarks home and they talked as they rode along. John I know you don't remember me but I was real good friends with your Father. That is why I bought the company so that when you became a man you could take over and run it. That is what your Father would have wanted said Mr. Clark. I don't know what to say but thank you said John. As you know I have cancer and have only six weeks or less to live and the only thing I ask is that you and Brandi let me live here in the house until I die. If it is ok with you I will turn over everything to you tomorrow said Mr. Clark. Sure said John. About that time they drove up in front on the big mansion and "they were greeted by the butler. Who's name was Sirling. Sirling this is Miss Brandi Mitchell and Mr. John Martin show them to their room. Yes sir if you will follow me. Will you be, needing two rooms sir asked Sirling? No please put everything in one room said John. Yes sir if should you need anything let me know and I will get it for you said Sirling. So they went with Sirling and he took them to their room and they got a crib for Courtney to sleep in. Then they came back down and Mr. Clark said make your self at home I have got to go and rest now I will see you at dinner. So John and Brandi and Courtney spent the afternoon down on the beach playing. That evening they met Mr. Clark for dinner and it was a great meal and all of them was, tired and so John Brandi and Courtney went up to their room and took a shower and went to bed. As they lay their talking Brandi said tomorrow is the big day. Yea the day I become a Multibillionaire and get my daddy's company back. There is something I need to tell you princess I love you John said smiling. I love you too said Brandi. And they went on off to dream land. The next morning they woke up to the smell of toast bacon and eggs and hash browns cooking. So they got dressed and came down. Brandi John and Courtney came down and said good morning everyone. Good morning sir. How did you and the Madam sleep asked Sirling? Great we slept like a log said John. Very good sir said Sirling. Good morning said Mr. Clark. Good morning sir said Sirling Brandi and John. John after breakfast we will sign those papers and turn everything over to you said Mr. Clark. Yes sir said John. How did you two sleep last night asked Mr. Clark? Great we slept like a log sir said John. I was hoping that you and Brandi would get a goodnight's sleep. So after breakfast John and Mr. Clark went in his study and sign the paper's giving John control of his Father's company. They spent the rest of that day with Mr. Clark. And that evening Brandi Courtney and John went down to the beach and sat down. And he started to thank about how it all got started.